# Persuasion's Price

**By Sam Grant**

Published by Sam Grant

Publishing partner: Paragon Publishing, Rothersthorpe
© Sam Grant 2019

ISBN 978-1-78222-687-1


Book design, layout and production management by Into Print
www.intoprint.net
+44 (0) 1604 832149

# Foreword

John Ledley farmer, has three lock up barn buildings cleared of bales. Opportunity to lease the barns arrives with a call from his estate agents. That the agents have vetted the new leaseholders reassures John.

Taras Kedrov arrives at John's farm with Izabella and son Anton. John is delighted that his barn's will be out on lease. Contracts are soon exchanged. Taras Kedrov, has a developed drug network, in an Asian overseas market, which has previously been built from gold smuggled into the UK. Sold discretely to jewellers and industrial users. But, Taras is a qualified marine engineer and has started a "nearly" legitimate valve engineering company. Izabella, his young partner, has developed an online cosmetics and fashion business. With many small businesses closed in the aftermath of the great recession the market town of Brodham needs rejuvenation.

Taras's son Anton has grown up in the UK. His mother Alsa, left Taras to escape a gangster environment and brought her son with her twenty – six years earlier. She has suffered ill-health in recent years and now lives with a sister, but is hospitalized.

Anton, has met up with father and they are on reasonably good terms, but he deplores the gangster life style. He is an established investment fund owner. Achieved through a successful career as a fund manager with a larger group. He wants his father to reform, but is now caught up with the group's activity. Unexpectedly, an opportunity arrives when his father is given an ultimatum. Izabella, however, is in need of investment to finance her business more effectively. An opportunity presents itself.

## A Work of Fiction

Brodham and West Frampton are fictional town and village set in the south west of England for purposes of the novel. Zircon Distribution Fund is also a fictional creation.

# Chapter 1

# A Market Town

Brodham was a market town. Local excitement could be a bullock that jumped a fence to escape market. Then, it might career up the high street and startle pedestrians. Perhaps in mimicry of Spanish cousins. One or two cars might suffer dents. Brodham Weekly Post, would then capture a photo shoot of a bullock cornered and fenced at the end of the high street. Not that frequent an event, but each time it re-ignited debate about market relocation to a field away from town. Critics pointed back to medieval historic significance. Farmers, were agreed, however, that the busy town centre made the beasts frisky and stressed. That, a field site on the edge of town would be better for all concerned. Maybe, though not for farmers wives, who were probably keen to be in town. After all, money changed hands at auction and husbands might be romanced toward a spend in the town shops.

Danny was an observer and participant. Not in the delivery and collection remit alone, but prescriptions were taken to town chemists; papers and sometimes groceries delivered to the home of an ailing villager. In-extremis notes inside a paying in book taken back by the post person, because the villager could not get into Brodham's bank. None of these errands, a role envisaged by Royal Mail for its employee. There were strategic stops for tea or coffee on Danny's rural delivery and where deliveries were made in good time, inevitably a wait on the clock was required. Post boxes needed to be cleared on time or later than the listed time, otherwise a prominent resident's complaint would lead to a reprimand. Inevitably, you might say, a post person would be regaled with goings on, in and around a local farm or village. Knowledge, more intimate, at times, than available to actual families, by virtue of familiar meet up with someone, untied to concerns, in the way that friends and family could be. Also, in Danny's case willing and able to help out after a day or two of fine weather at harvest time. He would field requests from Dot, like, 'Could you help out for a couple of afternoons Danny? John's well behind and now Luke's fell and broke his arm.' These occasions might be when Vicky, was home on the farm, in the summer. Danny, unlikely to refuse when Vicky's face would break into a smile, the moment he agreed to assist her father. 'It's straightforward tractor work, Danny. John says he's happier with your tractor skills, any day than when Luke's in the fields.' It was flattery, on Dot's part, but Danny readily agreed to help.

An agricultural landscape meant that several farms received daily van deliveries-sometimes with only one or two letters. Sub post office's known to inveigle a driver to deliver newspapers to a farm with reward of coffee. Farms, carved into an agricultural landscape made up of fields, barns, and lanes, best traversed by tractor or on horse- back. House outcrops boasted of village status - when hamlet would be closer to the mark. Linton Farm was a postal stop in a delivery which comprised eight villages. Landmark sites with a dozen or so cottages could include a sub post office, pub, and church. A cottage front room equipped with postal scales with a desk counter and lockable drawers to hold stamps and cash, in several of those hamlets, masquerading as villages.

Every sub-postmistress, if she were to enter TV's, "who wants to be a millionaire," with question content about village, and inhabitants, could, easily secure the million - pound jackpot prize. Annette Hastings post mistress at West Frampton bought a cottage with post office, attached a year previously. It came with paddock and stables in need of repair for the return of Cleopatra and foal. Opportunity to go riding was not as she'd hoped and plans were considered for a sale of the mare. Incorporated in a large field was a concreted free- standing area just off from Churchill Lane which could be let out to those with motor homes, holidaying in the area. Booked online with advance payment.

Although, relatively new to the life of a postmistress Annette was well on the way to acquisition of knowledge intrinsic to that role of sub postmistress, in a small village or hamlet.

~

It was six-thirty. Danny knew that by seven the van's interior light would no longer be needed to read names and addresses. Deceptively, the van was rammed with packages. Twenty of these were destined for the conservatory at 21, Oxton Road, in Church Frampton. A delivery and collection point for an online mail order company. An agreement locally by friends in the village. Psychologically, at least, for Danny, it was felt that progress was made, once this large consignment of packages no longer filled the van. Firstly, there was a call at Higham Lodge Farm. An open front door enabled the letter bundle to be poked into the wire cage behind without need to push open a heavy hinged flap. Rex, the Alsatian ran out to bite at the wheels of the van as Danny slowed, before the turn into Oxton Road. Perhaps, Darwin-like he'd developed an instant hostility toward the red postal van. A daily ritual. Where there was mail for the house a beep on the horn might elicit a call of 'Rex, you're not to play with the van, come inside.' Rex would obediently run back through the garden to the back door. Then made safe to open the van door. Twenty-one Oxton Road's conservatory was at the back entrance and some distance from Rex's house. Three trips from van to conservatory saw the van nearly clear of packages. After Oxton Crescent there was a ribbon strip of houses which led out of Church Frampton and into West Frampton. Then a small bundle of letters for Linton Farm.

# Chapter 2

# Anton, Taras and Izabella

'Whoever owns one of them?' Asked Luke, a late arrival in the farm house kitchen.

'What's that Luke?' Came back Dot's call. With, 'Get yourself sat down.'

Dorothy and John Ledley ran Linton Farm with a mainly Eastern European work force, with foreman in the summer months.

Luke was their latest young farm worker, in need of supervision. Not slow to give his opinion about the arrival in the yard of visitors

'That customized Range Rover. Not seen a fancy job like that in these parts.

'I'll see to them,' said John, who got up from his chair by the inglenook and placed the Farmers Weekly on the kitchen table. Speed with which he left the kitchen, broken with a backward step to snatch his cap, from its hook behind the farmhouse door, indicated that he was keen to meet these anticipated visitors. Several minutes later he called back from outside,

'Dorothy.' John's recourse to Dorothy, indicated the visitors were of importance.

Dot, poured Luke's mug of tea and placed the pot down, removed her apron and placed it over a chair. Stopped momentarily, to free and straighten tied - back hair in front of the inglenook wall mirror and was near the door before anyone entered from the outside cobbled farm yard and barns. Luke stood up to manage a better view from the sunken floored kitchen area.

'You mustn't mind us. We have a late breakfast on account of early morning work. Getting feed out, that sort of thing. Not like normal folk really,' said Dot. Three visitors followed John into the large hallway which was really part of the main kitchen, on account of work benches and burners to boil pans of milk plus an egg packing area. The older visitor said,

'No Mrs Ledley, that is so good for us, this- what is you can say – for us to see authentic way of life? Not. Like in the busy city, with noise and hurry everywhere.' Tall, dark, slicked haired, with grey threads at the sides. This extended to a combed more white than black front wave of hair, which transmitted that distinguished older man persona. A black suit with lightly silvered lines, cuff linked shirt, striped tie plus highly polished brogues. An out of place appearance for this rural setting. Dot looked at her husband for introductions, but the visitor made his own.

'Taras, Taras Kedrov. My partner Izabella is with me and my son Anton.' A wave in their direction was made before he shook hands with John and Dot.

'Hello, to you both,' continued Anton, who reached out, to shake both hands, like his father. Izabella managed a brief smile, but her eyes were more occupied with the new surroundings.

'John, you'd best show our guests into the front room.' A room only occupied on a Sunday and when guests arrived.

'Perhaps, you would like some tea. I have some made?' She turned to Taras, who smiled and said.

'That would be very welcome.'

They were now stood in the middle of the hall, which approached the kitchen area and open plan stairway.

Vicky walked downstairs, unobserved. Stopped brushing her hair, on hearing voices, but discreetly placed the hair brush between the rails of the banister. Eyes, directed toward Anton. Dot, on seeing Vicky smiled, and said,

10

'Vicky, we have visitors.'

'Your daughter?' Taras, asked.

'Yes, Vicky is home from college,' said John.

'That is delightful. My son Anton he went to school and university, here in England when I first arrived.' Anton responded to this.

'My father would like to think he is English, but's still a Russian refugee who cannot return,' Taras, shrugged his shoulders.

'I could if I wished to,' and smiled at Dot. Vicky caught the disparaging look from Anton, who was by his father's side. She was taken by the strong jaw and English voice with no foreign inflection. Obvious in his father's attempt at pronounced English. Strong dark features articulacy ignited allure for Vicky who admired, loved her Father. But one mainly taciturn male figure, in her life, was more than adequate. Izabella was not that much older than Anton, who was in his mid-twenties.

'I would be more interested to see outside. The farm around the house, yes,' said Izabella. The men always talk business. Would that be possible?' she asked. Dot replied.

'Perhaps, we could have tea and then,' she glanced at Vicky, 'afterwards, my daughter could show you around the outside. There's a mare with a foal.' Vicky didn't look enthusiastic, but gave her mother a weak smile, which strengthened when she turned toward Izabella.

'That would be really nice of you,' said Izabella. I didn't want at first to visit here, but now I feel happy.'

'That is as I expected cherie. I knew you would enjoy seeing the farm, once we were here,' said Taras, who wanted to please his younger partner, whenever possible. Already he'd help finance Izabella's online business. They'd met in London a year ago, but long after his first marriage broke down.

It would be difficult to envisage the existence of John and Dot Ledley's front room, unless you were either shown a photo or made a visit. Even the television in the corner looked ripe for a museum. A worn suite of furniture complemented faded velvet curtains. Photos on the mantlepiece were of Vicky sat up waving from a push chair, mounted in a silver frame. Then in school uniform, and after graduation, before she started studies for her Masters. On the far right a photo of Barabas. A bull with a large blue and white rosette. John, in a white coat held, a silver cup for best breed in the county, July 21$^{st}$, 2019.

'Magnificent beast. May I?' Taras got a nod from John, before he reached and picked up the photo frame, which he angled to catch the light. They were now in the front room. Anton smiled when Vicky pointed a finger at herself with his father's mention of a magnificent beast.

Photos occupied three quarters of the mantle shelf. Dot, however, was anxious to get her guests settled, and at ease.

'Izabella, perhaps you would like to sit in the chair nearest the window?' She said.

'Yes. That I would like. To see out into the farmyard.' She pointed across before she sat down.

'I see the mare with its head out of the stable. She is more beautiful than the bull.' It was said to get Taras's attention. That he required to be informed by Izabella when her presence did not receive sufficient attention.

'They are both beautiful animals, cherie,' said Taras.

'The mare, is stabled here. That's Cleopatra,' said Dot. 'Now we have a foal to look after. Do sit down everyone.' Vicky and Anton choose the settee. John directed Taras to the armchair opposite. Dot, in turn, smiled to herself before she left to fetch teas, because Vicky got up and adjusted the photos of her in the pram and school uniform, away from view on the mantlepiece. Anton queried her decision.

'What's wrong?' They're good photos of you' Anton said. 'Better than mine, when a baby and child.' Taras and John, continued to talk un-noticing, although Vicky stepped between the two of them. Vicky decided otherwise about the photos. Dot shut the front room door and waved at Luke, to get him on the move.

'You can go back to work Luke. John will be a little while, yet,' she said and placed the kettle back on the hob before she went to the dresser to remove floral patterned cups and matching teapot.

'Who are they Mrs Led?' asked Lucas as he got up from the chair.

'They're customers. But it's none of your business is it Luke?'

'Your Vick was quick down those stairs.'

'And what do you mean by that Luke?'

'Nothing really, but we don't get posh people like those here that often. And well perhaps they're more like the sort she meets, at college.'

'Fancy clothes and cars can be all show, you know Luke.'

'I wouldn't mind a bit of that show, though Mrs Led.'

'Well, you'd better get out to work, then hadn't you?' said Dot, as Luke made for the door in his stockinged feet.

# Chapter 3

# Barns Meet with Approval

John received a succinct message from agents, Turnbull & Atkins, a week earlier.

'Did he have barns available for storage? How many? And could they send a valued client to have a look?" That was if John had spare capacity. Last season's hay was sold a few weeks back. It was a positive "Yes," from John and that there were three barns available and a paddock for good measure.

'Alright for next Wednesday then Mr Ledley?' came back the email.

'Mid-morning. It'll need to be before midday. Can't sit around all day, you know.' To that extent a visit from Tara, partner and son was not unexpected.

'And you're wanting barn rental to store for three months, with access for a small work force? Asked John.

'Small work force, only, with infrequent delivery and dispatch.'

'How frequent? I mean how many times a week? The road can't take too much traffic,' enquired John.

'Once a month at most. That's after the main first delivery,' said Taras. It will be a store house to replenish premises in Brodham.

'Perhaps, father, we can assist to strengthen the road for extra traffic.' Anton was keen to secure the deal to get his father settled. John's eyes lightened at the suggestion.

Prospects for this deal was getting better by the minute. Dot placed the tea tray on the nearby table.

'I understand from the agents that there are three available. We would like to have a few packing tables in the third barn away from the farm building. Not that there will be noise. Mainly, the space will be to store crates of machinery, but the packing space will be made for some cosmetic product. We will hire portacabin facilities for staff and toilets, if you are in agreement?

'That shouldn't be a problem – provided these are regularly serviced,' said John.

'But of course. There will be some crates with tableware, books and Izabella's clothing and shoes that she has never unpacked.' Izabella interrupted.

'No, because nowhere have we lived that was suitable for me to unpack properly, Taras, you make it that it is somehow my fault?'

'No cherie, I do not. It is just what you say just life?' He looked across at John who smiled sympathetically.

'The third barn has a paddock which is unused. Did the agents mention that this was also available?'

'Yes. I have seen the rental amounts for the barns and paddock, which are what I would expect to pay. I will pay three months in advance to the agent. If that us agreeable?' John impressed with the offer, said

'That's fine Mr Kedrov. That's just fine.'

Dot wanted everything to proceed without frisson and turned to Izabella to include her.

'Do you take milk, sugar, Izabella?'.

'Just milk, no sugar and so too for Taras, when he is with me.'

'Anton?' Dot's call broke into Vickys's laugh, which came out of some remark Anton made about his father.

'The same for me Mrs Ledley, if that's all right?'

'Vicky, perhaps you'd like to see to Anton?' Vicky continued talking but stood after her mother placed Taras's and Izabella's cups of tea on the coffee table in front of the inglenook. She sat on the settee next to Izabella, who talked about how she

15

missed her home town of Vladivostok and about her father in the Russian navy. When Izabella got up to place her cup and saucer back on the table Vicky asked,

'Would you like to have a look outside?'

'Yes, that would be very nice,' she sat, again. A raised leg, purportedly to inspect the flow of skin-tight leggings, failed in its primary objective to attract Anton's attention.

'I'm ready for some fresh air. Anton, you will also be wanting to come with us to look at the mare and its foal. You are a horseman. Is that not so?

'You know I would like to Izabella, but I need to stay as father's translator.' Taras, wasn't amused and broke off from talking with raised eyebrows. Anton, waved and nodded his head and said,

'Just joking.' Dot held the tray, assisted by Anton, who returned the cups and saucers from table to tray.

'You can take Izabella through the French windows Vicky,' said Dot. Double-glazed, they led out into the yard.

'I'll so miss Cleopatra and the foal when they return to their owner,' said Vicky.

'Who is that?' Asked Izabella as she followed Vicky,

'They belong to the sub postmistress, at West Frampton.'

The sound of a tractor could be heard after Vicky left the door ajar. John stood up went across to his desk next to the French windows and removed plans from a drawer. Returned, and spread these on the table. Each diagram showed top elevation layout for individual barns. Floor space varied, because they were each constructed when the Ledley's finance allowed, by different builders.

'Turnbull's, said you wanted to store crates which are one metre tall with a floor width of a metre and a quarter?'

'There're ten which are twice that size, but mainly they're the same, as you say,' said Taras.

'It's a mixture of belongings. There're equipment and

supply parts for my valve supply company and a consignment of cosmetics. These are the important part.'

'I wouldn't let Izabella hear you say that,' said Anton.

'Never mind that, but remind me to run through the manifest with you Anton.' Understanding of the significance of the items to be stored known only to the two of them. Associates were paid well not to ask questions.

A squawking from ducks came through the open door with mail van's approach. Dixie, the collie shot out from where she lay to welcome Danny, who stopped near to where Izabella was being nuzzled by the mare. Linton Farm was a break, in the delivery round. Dan, usually served himself, from the pale green enamelled coffee pot Taras looked at John enquiringly.

'It's all right it's only the postman, Dorothy will see to him. You're wanting the barns on three month contract. How many crates of each size?'

Five hundred in total, of the smaller ones. One hundred of larger crates. My lorries will deliver here. Do you have a fork lifter John?'

'Yes, we can stack the crates on the walls of the first barn there are rows of racking. That's if you're happy to pay for us to do it. Would fifty pounds an hour be acceptable?'

'Yes. That is not a problem.'

'Hadn't we better have a look father?' Asked Anton.

'Yes, I was going to suggest that,' said John. They're relatively new build. Did Turnbull and Atkins show you the interior photos?'

'I have worked out the storage availability,' said Anton, 'and we should manage with two barns and three – quarters to allow space for conveyor belt, machinery and trestles. There's a mains supply, I understand?' Anton asked John.

'That's right. I will take a reading with you or a representative before you start and at the end. Agric-Electric, our suppliers will bill you for this reading, if that's alright.'

'My son is right, of course. I have seen the photos of the interiors, but it's best that we see them for ourselves.'

'I'll show you around, then,' said John. He went out of the room to see Dot, who kept the keys to everything on the inner wall of the inglenook. They had to be returned at the end of each day. An inspection of all three barns was made by Taras and Anton, queried that odd pieces of machinery were in the corner of the first barn, but told by John that they would be moved before contracts were signed. On their return Izabella and Vicky were back.

'It is a good horse to ride, then?' Izabella asked Vicky

'Cleopatra, is the best. We get on very well. We understand each other.'

'Females of all species can often do this, I think. But the horse and foal are to go back with the owner?'

'Yes, unfortunately. I will miss Cleopatra and her foal.' Said Vicky.

'We will be ready to go soon Izabella.'

'I have no intention of cooking,' responded Izabella.

'Have you tried the Trellis and Vine, in town,' said John. They do a range of bar food and main course.'

'That sounds like a good idea,' said Izabella. 'You can book a table Taras.'

'I will do that cherie, if that is what you would like,' said Taras before he returned to discuss rental for the barns.

'I would like to have Anton return to finalize the deal. These white concrete floors will be needed to be chalked for the layout when our delivery managers are here to receive the deliveries.'

'Of course, that's fine, Mr Kedrov. That's no problem. Anton can come anytime. Just call us on this number a day in advance. John handed a card with the address of Linton Farm to Anton. Taras asked

'Do you have the phone number for this Trellis and

Vine? Or web address, perhaps,' said Anton.

'Yes,' from his wallet John produced a card with a surround of green vine leaves.

'No, it's alright,' you can have that one, we've plenty others round and about. After their departure he said to his wife,

'That commission we paid to Turnbull and Atkins has been a good investment in the way things have turned out.'

# Chapter 4

# Annetta Hastings

There was no need to go out into the street to water the flower boxes, because they could be reached through the opened windows. Miss Hastings, Annetta or plain Etta to friends knew that the curate's flat overlooked not only the graveyard, but also, West Frampton post office. Annetta found out that he was fifty, to that of her thirty two. A discovery made whilst she talked with the vicar, after church.

'That Latin dance membership is restricted to those under sixty. Mr Daniels your curate might he be interested to get to meet people socially? Will he be in an age range for the dance group? She asked. It's for the under sixties, vicar?' she made this point, in the hope that the vicar would reveal his age.

'Yes, now that sound like a good idea Etta. Mr Daniels, Peter, is fifty. He gets under that bar, you might say.' That was the answer she wanted and quickly followed up with.

'We've a new meeting next Tuesday. A first lesson is two pounds. Maria has said it's a taster, for starters to find out if they've energy for Latin. Further lessons will be five pounds.'

'It would be a good opportunity for him to meet members of the congregation, in the raw, so to speak. I'll have a word with Peter. Annetta, blushed, unexpectedly when Christina said the word raw. Now thirty five, but Annette never wrestled with the question of whether to have children or not. Two young sisters Penelope and Felicity, both names abbreviated to Penny and Flic had previously popped a combined brood of five. A role of aunt she performed dutifully, but was always relieved when a sister, in question, received the child or children back again.

Her sub post office had been financed by a short sale of shares on the London stock market. Financial experience brought into use from younger days whilst employed by a London bank. Money making machine the post office wasn't. Annetta, also accepted commissions through the sale of ebay items from local farmers wives and had even been known to sell the occasional tractor or automated stacking machine or such-like for a singleton farmer with ten per cent commission

Neatly dressed in a trouser suit when she attended to postal business, Annetta had taken to variations of dress and short skirt when she stepped outside to water the flower boxes morning and evening. A curate would need to be a vicar before he met Annetta's requirement at a social level, if she were to be his wife, that is, but it was an opportunity to make herself visible at ground floor level, so to speak.

Today, being Monday after the door was unbolted, top and bottom and the blind let up to reveal an open sign, she picked up her mobile and called Mavis, at West Frampton post office

'Has he left yet?' she asked. 'Danny isn't it?' Annetta always hoped the postman would arrive early. The squire and sometimes the vicar could pop in with letters or to make cash transactions. It was inappropriate to have working people in the post office when she needed to give immediate attention to these important local people.

'Oh, yes a few minutes ago, replied Mavis. 'How's that new curate settling in Etta?'

'I wouldn't really know,' she said. 'I've only just talked about him with the vicar.'

'Just wondered. He's down for taking the service in East Frampton in a month's time. I suppose I'll have to wait 'til then.'

'Yes, you will,' said Annetta 'I'll see you at the WI on Tuesday, Mavis. Goodbye.'

Annetta, placed her mobile under the counter. She needed

to prepare documents for Danny after he first cleared the post box, set into the ivied wall outside Annetta's experiences of her sisters' partners led to the conclusion that younger men were needy and likely to require over much management. She recognized that several young business gentleman who would normally send an office secretary with the mail, were attracted. Two had been rejected for a date, but still visited. Annetta was not an unpollinated flower. Subconsciously, to these men this might have been a reason further allure. Women, as has been said, love to position a man at their mercy. Annetta was no exception. But, an ongoing relationship with a younger partner meant demands which could lead to an unrequired pregnancy. Annetta was comfortable with pill taking, but in short bursts of expediency. A man, particularly a younger one, could not be trusted, she believed, to practice good contraception technique.

Annetta, though, knew how to interest a single or married man, of fifty five. Flirtatious smiles, with meaningful intent, might be displayed thirdly. Suitors at the post office never saw the flicker of eyelids, that tremble in the eyes nor winsome smile. Jeans, when worn offered opportunity to display a raised leg and toes pointed, which drew attention to a coquettish presentation when she saw possibilities of a true knight and potential protector from predation with unplanned conquest, you could say. After introductory chat, the smile might disappear to denote that she was open for conversations about those risky topics, like religion and politics, but not sex. Energetic talk, which could determine whether a man was prepared to act and react with questions directed in her interests.

A well-developed smile would become a prime position, which indicated that the male recipient was on Annetta's dance list, though the music was yet to start. Resultant successful acceptance could release play of that third mentioned component, a smile with distinct flirtatious intent. A Latin dance class suggested to Annette a more rapid assessment of knight aptitude obtained at an early stage. The Maria Agrande's Dance School was run by Beverly Arkwright. Students were encouraged to address Beverly as Maria, a former stage name. Hire of the church hall was fifty pounds. Ideally thirty dancers were required to cover costs and leave a little profit for Beverly. It was really more a show case for her weekday dance studio in town than a fully-fledged business. Customarily, more women students than men, which meant one or other would dance the male role. Project progression from the previous year was made, in that a pair of disabled wheel chair users with some degree of mobility had enrolled. Peter, curate, after enrolment, at the vicar's suggestion said he would partner one or other of them for at least one dance. Both wheel chair dancers relied on support, and were well proportioned. There partner needed both strength and you could say catchability, should they lose balance when attempts were made to perform Latin dance routines.

# Chapter 5

# Meeting Room Organized

Taras, called to book a table before they left Linton Farm. He also made a call, at the end of their meal, to two Associates.

'We can talk about the plans for the barns when at the Pub, Oleg. Yes, we have three barns for storage. It is problem solved. Yes, you can bring Maya with you.' A pause.

'Yes, Yakov with Tamara. They are still together? You are to speak English at all times you understand? We are from Slovakia, if anyone should ask. Yes, yes, Poland's all right. It's perhaps even better. We must not mention Russia, Oleg. They see Russians all as spies with nerve poison.

'Yes, they might still be suspicious of Germans. But so, am I Oleg, you know? They're arrogant when they know you're from Russia. These English country people are not so fussy , and when they've been paid, they are not so disliking of us. I will expect you in one hour's time, then. Bring the manifest with you, okay. Goodbye.' Izabella made her feelings felt.

'Do we have to have business discussed, even when we go for a meal, Taras?'

'We can perhaps find a room upstairs, Izabella.'

'And I will talk with Tamara and Maya about the latest fashion in London and Moscow.' Izabella's whisper was barely audible, when she turned to look across to where Anton was by the bar 'I cannot, though, have Anton to myself,' she said in a disappointed whisper. Her eyes lit up, when Anton turned to walk back from the bar with a tray of drinks.

'It's on a tab, father,'

'That's okay. Anton can you go back and ask the girl at the bar if you can speak with the Landlord?'

'But she will most likely have a boyfriend,' Izabella remarked, as she reached to take a second vodka martini from the tray. Anton ignored that remark.

'Oleg and Yakov, will be arriving shortly. I think it is best you ask the landlord for a room to meet. He will have no suspicions when you ask with your English gentleman's voice.

'Not that of a Russian thug,' said Izabella, which Taras ignored.

'What time? For how long? How much?' Asked Anton.

'From two thirty will be okay. Suggest a fifty pound payment. I would manage it for less, but they will want to overcharge, because of the way you speak.' Anton didn't question this.

'Anton, your father is only jealous. It is appealing to people that you speak, well. You've a good education and have your own business in the City. Especially I find this so,' her coquettish smile made no impression on Anton who was already on his way to the bar. Carol, the bar maid/waitress called the Landlord before she came across to take orders for coffee.

'Cappuccino,' said Izabella. 'I would like a Cappuccino.'

'I will have an Americano?'

'With Milk?'

'Yes. Make it two.' Taras ordered the same for Anton.

Carol, tapped the pad and stood back when George, the Landlord and Anton arrived.

'Mr Kedrov?'

'Yes,' Said Taras. Anton's adopted British name was Carter, but either might have answered.

'Mr Kedrov, we have a room for your meeting. It's number seven, on the landing above the stairs.' He pointed across to the far corner of the lounge bar. A varnished bannister was visible at the end of an oak panelled strip decorated with brass horse medallions, which led to a landing. George Parry, a red-faced landlord wore a white apron which suggested that he had been called from the pub kitchen.

'It is ready whenever you require use of it. Up until four. I have a Ladies Guild meeting from five until seven and we need to prepare the room.

'It's not then a bedroom?' asked Taras. George, smiled politely, in the way he might in answer to Anton's chauffeur, if he had one.

'It was,' said George, 'a large double bedroom, but there's a large function room across the yard. For small meetings we decided to convert number seven into a small business room, you see. It has a table and eight chairs with a flat screen TV, broadband connection; kettle, tea and coffee making facilities. Perhaps you would like to take a look?' Anton, before he returned to the conversation looked at his father, who nodded.

'I expect it will be ideal,' he said. There are not that many of us, but we will have a look. After coffees.' With the room key in his left hand George first placed it on a tray

'There is the key.' He placed key and tray on the table in front of Anton.

'Carol will bring you your coffees.' As he spoke the dimpled glass door, which led into the main bar opened.

'Ah, there is the postman, I am expecting a parcel from Amazon. So glad I caught him. I hope you will find number seven adequate to your needs, sir. See to the coffee orders. Carol please,' he said before he walked over to meet up with Danny.

The Trellis and Vine, was Danny's last call for the day. A final wall box, was cleared outside the pub before return to Brodham's retail park's main delivery office.

# Chapter 6

# Vicky Confides in Cleopatra

It was outside the stable after the visit from Anton when Vicky was mucking out the stable that she decided to confide with the mare about how she met up by chance with him.

'He asked me out Cleopatra.' Her father referred to Cleopatra as Cleo, but this trivialized the magnificence of the mare in Vicky's eyes. A text message was sent after they exchanged numbers when Anton visited with his father and Izabella.

'He asked me out, but sort of not yet. You see he's helping his father with a consignment of parts for his engineering firm.' The mare whinnied, which nicely chimed with Vicky's attempt to express her feelings out loud, but not so that anyone else could hear. A hand stroked the white streak that flowed from the mare's head down to the moist of the nostrils.

Home from taking her finals, university would soon be a memory. There was a struggle to get a thesis in and now seemed a good moment to look for relaxation and some down time. That meant escape from a strict focus on music study and the role of counterpoint in the composition of orchestral works, which she found uninteresting, even depressing.

'He plays the trumpet.' He said this in reply to her question as to which instrument, he played.

This followed from her answers about what she studied. Music combined with art history. So glad that music was the other half of the degree course. However, brilliant Leonardo's last supper undoubtedly was, after a few minutes of sitting in a lecture hall staring at the slide of this or another renaissance painting, Vicky found herself fighting to keep her eyes open.

'And I play the violin. Well that's the instrument I've played the most.' She said. For choice I'd most like to be a drummer in a rock band.' Anton smiled.

'Either works well alongside a trumpet. With suitable music, of course.' He said.

'It's definitely got possibilities.'

They'd scored a connection. Why didn't she ever meet a guy like Anton at university, but they were young students, who were all finding their way.

'We're going to the Trellis and Vine for lunch,' he went on to say, Cleopatra.

'I know that pub, I said and Say hello to Carol for me. She usually works behind the bar.' Why on earth did I mention Carol and then follow it up with 'We used to go riding together before I left for uni. It's not a mystery is it Cleopatra? But why did I even say that?' Carol was married with a three year old now. Vicky sought solace in her chat with Cleopatra where a serious relationship was nowhere on the radar. Well, not as she viewed things. Anyhow, Anton could be separated with five children for all she knew. She considered that he needed to be separated, divorced or straightforwardly unmarried to suggest they meet up.

'It's terrible, what we have to put up with Cleopatra. Where's that stallion now?' An opened hand revealed a sugar lump which ensured Cleopatra's continued attention. 'when we're kept on the hook. He has my number and suggested that perhaps he could call when the storage was complete, and that I had no plans to stay on the farm. Yes, I did say that Cleopatra. It's not totally true, but I want him to get back. Not so that I become another number on his phone menu. No, I don't want to leave you, either.' Her hand stroke increased in pressure to reassure herself, as much as Cleopatra.

'Vicky! Your phones got a new chime. Did you know it sounds like it's playing the Trumpet Voluntary?'

When she reached the farm door Vicky took the phone from her mother.

'Hi, Vicky!' She recognized Carol's voice on her phone. A school friend from way back. There was non stop talk and it was all about Anton. But Carol needed to cut Vicky off.

# Chapter 7

# The Meeting

Customers were arriving, at the Trellis and Vine. A heart effect made by the twisted vine across the window gave Carol a view outside. Two suited men in dark glasses followed by a fair and darker haired woman walked towards the entrance. Both women wore skinny jeans, but carried handbags of a quality not associated with any of the Frampton villages. Carol decided to call George, and end her chat.

'You'll have to stop there now Vicky,' from Carol who did most of the talking.

When Carol asked Vicky if she was attracted to Anton, the reply back was,

'What makes you think that?' A stifled yawn a bit on the theatrical side followed.

'They're just business people Carol, who want to rent barn space from father. You just have to be friendly, nothing more.'

'Bye then,' said Carol, who swiped her phone and slipped it into a crumpled excuse for a handbag before the guests reached the bar. Oleg, Taras's associate was doing the talking.

'It's all right, Izabella is here. I do not believe you'll have nothing to say you three together.

What you think Yakov?' He asked. Yakov, caught sight of Taras, plus Izabella and Anton seated on a table on the far side of the lounge bar and waved to acknowledge their arrival. Oleg approached the bar. Carol placed a wiped glass back under the bar, smiled and said

'Hi,'

'Yes, Hi. We would like.' He turned to Maya and Tamara.

'What do you like to drink?'

'I will have a white wine, said Maya to Oleg

'Mine is a ginger and soda,' said Tamara. 'We will be with Izabella,' she added and they left, Oleg and Yakov to order and pay for drinks.

'White wine and ginger and soda and for you?' Asked Carol.

'Half a bitter,' chimed Yakov. Carol pointed to the brass polished pump handles.

'Whichever is the best bitter. I will have a half, as well,' said Oleg.

'Frampton original is popular and a best bitter.' Carol pointed to the third pump along.

'That's okay.' Carol placed the drinks when prepared on a tray. Oleg, paid and sipped his half pint before he walked across. Yakov, left to carry the tray to the table.

'Good evening Izabella, said Oleg. To be in accord with Oleg, Yakov nodded.

'It may be good for you, but I could think of better things to do. When you go to the NEC for Taras be sure to make discreet enquiries for me, Yes?'

'What is that for cherie?'

'Just business contacts. There is a cosmetic display in another hall,' she said in a dismissive way. Taras lost interest when she mentioned this. But Oleg knew otherwise as to what the true meaning of the question was. Taras, stood up and said to the two of them,

'We can take our drinks upstairs,' and picked up the room key.

'We have a room reserved. It's number seven. You two can bring your drinks up with you. Taras and Anton got up and were followed by Oleg and Yakov up the stairs to the next floor.

'It is not bugged in here then?' asked Oleg after Taras closed the door.

'Why would it be?' said Taras. 'We have, just booked it and this is England. The only place they watch is on the roads and when you shop. They never know who is here in this country or not. There's every nation under the sun. But it is suspicious if we are seen to be Russian. I have told you that they are happy if you say you are Hungarian, Polish or even Romanian.

'We have a new manager at the Dulwich Hotel in Wimbledon,' said Oleg as they sat around the table.

'Why is that? Asked Anton. Taras's hotel provided accommodation for corporate directors and high- ranked diplomats who might pay for additional services, which meant that they never talked about the hotel. That both parties maintained a secrecy and protectiveness toward the other.

'We discipline staff in front of guests. They understand, it is a little play, but it reassures high status guests. They're made to feel secure when there're secrets, they want to hide.'

'A previous manager was heard to talk about a guest, a senior agent, in the bar. He became high risk to us all, you understand Taras and our valued guests, of course. It was unfortunate, but the repair sign not to use the lift was removed mid-afternoon next day. He was helped to walk into the lift's empty space on his way from his office to the ground floor. You could say he arrived more quickly than expected. Reception, said that they heard a scream followed by a thud.

'Has it been recorded as an accident? What has since happened asked Taras?'

'Oh yes. It is okay we'd made sure that a high level of barbiturate was in the body before autopsy. Cause of death was later recorded as misadventure. I talked with the coroner; you see. It was good, but bad, if you understand, that he had recently separated from his wife. He was a depressed man. So sad and we agreed. It was terrible and that his death pointed to suicide.'

'The new manager I hope has been well vetted?'

'Yes, he is previously from the civil service. He was in hospitality and it is good that he has signed their official secrets act, yes. He will keep secret whatever he hears. We are able to make regular customers build debt, but of course ensure they have funds to cover this. Additional services are available from the girls who work the casino. They're paid twenty per cent out of the payment, but it can be a struggle to pay the bills, even so.' Anton, planned to sell the Dulwich when possible, and didn't feel any sympathy for these two.

'Yakov,' continued Taras, 'you have information about the corridor through Europe for arms and drugs to incite a revolution in the outer areas of Italy. There is a plan to extricate gold from the bank vaults of Vatican City and Rome. I believe to finance the revolutionary force. We now have facilities to store ingots.'

'Yes, you are in a good position to do this Taras,' said Yakov.

'Father,' said Anton, his voice despairing in tone. 'You said that you were going legal once the valve engineering firm was set up. This sounds like craziness.'

'It will be held in the barns for a limited time in boxes marked up as engineering parts. No one will know otherwise. It is a business contract. And it will pay well.'

'I hope that is all you have in that warehouse. Gold in transit. Nothing else?'

'I told you Anton we are to go legit. There is a little cocaine, but for overseas. Izabella will have her online cosmetics business. I will be back to my first love for engineering. You see, Anton it has to be gradual.'

Anton wanted to believe that progress was being made toward his father becoming untangled from his past. He knew little about Izabella's background, who Taras had met at a business conference.

'Because, I know these people in Italy,' said Taras. 'It will be good. One last business deal with old friends. The gold is in London bank vaults, but it needs to be moved for transit.'

'Away from prying eyes in farm buildings,' you said. Yakov's English was the most correct. Taras, who was sitting at the head of the table with Anton on his right was quick to reassure him.

'We now have secured the farm storage. It is nearby.'

'A remote farm,' said Anton. I explained that we want you to be here to oversee the storage. You loaned a car for test approval from that London dealer?'

'Yes. They'll be disappointed when they know we do not want to buy it,' said Oleg.

'It's already bought for the company, here in Brodham. It doesn't need returning,' continued Anton.

'I've bought it through a holding company. We didn't want it to be connected to here.'

'You think of everything Anton,' said Taras.

'It's always necessary to plan ahead, father. Finance for your new build house has been secured and there'll be a warehouse to assemble high pressure undersea valves. We need to establish bona fide credentials for this business. You will be registered at company's house.

'This all sounds good Taras. We expect crates to be moved from London almost immediately.'

Taras looked toward Yakov for more details.

'It will be the beginning of next month. We, that's me and Oleg will remove the crates from the lorries with perhaps the farmer's assistance, as you suggested and will be there as company managers to ensure the crates are handled safely.'

'Yes, that is reasonable,' said Taras.

'I want ingot crates marked with this picture of a valve and with the company logo and marked "Extreme Depth Valves."' Taras, removed a cellophane covered photo from his jacket pocket.

'I have a PDF photo for re-production in the company stamp.' He showed the photo to Anton.

'Next time the crates will have genuine parts, father?' Taras didn't answer in the presence of Oleg and Yakov.

'Labels can be made up locally and attached on arrival of the crates before storage. You can organize this then. We will continue to build the buy to let portfolio. How many are there now Anton?

There are five and there's a new hotel in negotiation. I suggest that this property group, together with the London hotel is made into a limited company. If you are in agreement it will have a British name.'

'Have you any ideas?' Taras asked.

'How about Blackthorn. That's an English tree name, which can really only be British.

'Yes, that's good.' Taras nodded his head in agreement. Anton, wanted to wean his father off all nefarious activities and would have liked to sever connections with the likes of Oleg and Yakov. This was not going to happen overnight.

'Anton will look at the Dulwich's books in a months' time. These accounts need to go to the accountant. You'll need to cover both gambling and escort services with alternative expenditure by the guests.'

'That we already do,' said Yakov. We have West End theatres that give us receipts for tickets we have bought for guests. For women, also there is a health spa. Both are booked to play rounds of golf. And theatres like to make it seem that the seats are reserved to impress theatre critics. That is when they are not there to watch the show. It's helpful to record ticket sales, even when no one goes to watch, they say.'

'I didn't know you were so keen on the theatre,' said Anton.'

'Not me, it is Tamara. She like to be seen going to the theatre. And I have to show interest, you know,' replied Yakov. He looked toward Taras for sympathetic understanding.

'It was her idea to pretend we bought tickets and sold them to the guests. You know how it is Taras, it is best to keep a partner happy.'

'So,' continued Taras, in two weeks' time you two will be back here. You can contact Anton, okay?

'I need to attend local town business meetings. We want to be sure that they are convinced we are a valve and marine engineering supply company.'

'Which you are to be father!' Exclaimed Anton.

'Anton has prepared a list of companies that we will validate us if any checks are made.'

'You think of everything Taras,' said Oleg.

'Charity contributions will be made, of course, to maintain influence with important town's people. Anton you have put forward your name to run in the London marathon. Izabella tells me. The town will be impressed with this.'

'So, will I, if I'm fit enough to compete,' said Anton.

# Chapter 8

# Linton Farm

'Well are they taking the barns for storage?' asked Dot.

'Yep, I've got three months' rent in advance.' Dot and Vicky had been into Brodham in the early the afternoon. For John every day was that keeping an eye on the farm the cows milking and Luke. Later in the year the supervision of fruit picking and a seasonal work force.

'Annette's taken their cheque. It'll need to clear. Cheques are like part of a world that's fast disappearing. Son Anton said, he could transfer straight from his phone to my account. But father wanted to deposit a cheque and pay by monthly standing order. I've given a receipt. Prefer a cheque,' said John, with a shrug of his shoulders.

'And when do they need to move in then?' asked Dot. She didn't wait for an answer, but called out.

'Do you want what we're having?' Vicky was trying on a top, in front of the mirror, above the inglenook.

'Just, ham and salad. No chips or any of that gateaux.' Student life in the last year plus exams stress she realized, had contributed to weight gain.' John answered.

'They're moving crates early August, they say. Just got a call from Anton, the son. Before you returned. They want use of the forklift and will pay twenty pound an hour. More than cover Luke's wages. They're sending storage managers to supervise. Bet me and the lad could do it all with none of that palaver.'

'You'll want them out before December at the latest, John.'

'I know, but there's a three months penalty clause for not being out.'

'They know about that then do they?'

Yes, Turnbull and Atkins made it clear before they sent them over,' said John. 'It's a lucky break to have the barns leased out.'

'Did you see that Izabella?'

'No, what do you mean Dot? Asked John.

'What do I mean? Wouldn't trust that Taras's chances with her. She's already got eyes on the son, Although, he doesn't appear to notice. Very polite and assured young man. I kind of feel sorry for the lad with that rough diamond of a father.' Vicky, sat at the kitchen table, with ears like a bat picked up on this.

'Then you must know how it must be for me then,' and turned a page of Horse and Hound.'

'Your father's not in fine clothes all the time, if that's what you mean? That university's given you ideas.'

'No, only joking.'

# Chapter 9

# Anton Returns by Train

Anton left the meeting early for a Monday conference with the Transport Secretary. His Fund Zircon National Distribution aimed to secure a deal whereby clients could have access to investments which provided mobile meter - based charge machines in council held park space. Initially for a London district, but with possibilities of national coverage. Central government was trialling the project. Anton understood that the format was to have cameras attached to posts that communicated via radio frequency to an individual car. Payments ring- fenced locally meant better security plus electric vehicles received a thirty per cent discount. Phone payment method was not new, but central government were keen to secure contracts with a particular overseas company. Any spare council land, which awaited development, could then have meter- based machines and cameras in position to acquire revenue.

Private car park landlords would be able buy into the scheme. It was a simple idea, which with government assistance and Zircon's investment, on behalf of clients could be rolled out nationwide.

Anton relaxed in a first glass carriage with feet on the opposite seat whilst he scrolled through his screen to assimilate anything relevant to him with regard to the upcoming meeting.

A British education and the change of name from Anton Kedrov to Anthony Carter or Ant as he became known at school. In contradiction to a six- foot muscular frame, made him appear like a certainly close establishment figure, if not quite on that footing. His father's past and present he would've liked, when possible, hidden from view, where wealth, is important, but background and relations are also key criteria for acceptance in high places. Anton achieved the wealth status, plus impeccable references from university luminaries. Five years as a successful fund manager, before setting up on his own, showed a proven track record with no awkward questions likely about background. He was educated in Britain and dressed and talked appropriately with establishment school background. Influential school tie could be worn, should the occasion arise. Anton did not seek to deceive but understood that news about his ancestry might lead to discrimination, on the way to the higher pinnacles. Once there, it would be safe. British upper echelons known to embrace others, where wealth and power reside, although they abhorred those differences and eccentricity, when they appeared further down the social scale. In particular, the last thing Anton wanted was a "reveal," of father's business empire. Perhaps with a degree of naivety about this situation with regard to government sources.

When at his London office Anton would walk across the battery of screens, much like a Chess grand master who makes a move on each board, after quiet deliberation. Anton addressed each market index player by first name. Not averse to compliments to female associates, for example like,

'Love that perfume Kate-does it have a lemon base?'

Yes, this could be interpreted as unwanted harassment from a male colleague, but with Anton the young woman in question would show appreciation with a smile, where a work colleague would likely get a look that said

'What you want is not on offer!'

Or communicated verbally as clear off! But put more explicitly. All fifty associates were entered into a Friday lottery. Each occupied a numbered station. Individual numbers were entered into a red, yellow and green circle of intermittently lit numbers. The circle was accessible on their screens where the numbers lit and unlit through the week. Participants could then freeze the randomly lit colours of their choice. They paid five pounds each and Anton made the fund up to a main prize of five hundred pounds.

There were performance related monthly bonuses, but this gave everyone a chance to score with a prize win. About twenty associates might consistently outperform the market. Others just did not have that heady mixture of market savviness and you might say innate ability to calculate risk and back the odds successfully, but they were still regarded in the organization. It was about fostering a sense of team togetherness. Bonus performance associates would return their number. As luck would have it an associate could be awarded a bonus and also win the weekly lottery when bonuses were at an all- time high. That question, not always voiced, that perhaps success in life has an element of luck from birth.

Anton removed phone and leather wallet, which he placed on the table of the first- class compartment. A ticket inspector could be heard approaching. There were gaps of empty seats either side, but there was the distinct call of,

'Have your tickets ready please. Next stop is Kings Cross.' He removed a ticket from his suit jacket pocket ready for display to the inspector.

'Perfectly in order, sir,' said the inspector when he returned it to Anton.

'Will you be wanting a taxi from Kings Cross, sir? Do you live nearby?'

'I might,' replied Anton. A card was placed in front of him.

'If it's of any help my brother Steven can be there for you.' He looked at his watch, then continued.

'Save on the hassle. Nearly always a scramble around leaving work, you know. Just say that Tony mentioned it.

Anton looked at the white card with a silver serrated edge.

Steven Arbuthnot

Taxi and Hire.

Exclusive Wedding Service.

Mobile: 0117684320

'The card advertises weddings, but he does funerals as well, if you ask, that is. Just that he didn't like to have the word on the card. It might look sort of threatening, you see.'

'I'll certainly consider it. Very enterprising of you.'

'Thank you, sir. It's helpful both ways you might say. Don't mention it to the railway will you though. They'd not like it that I gave work to the competition, so to speak.'

'Yeah, I understand your point. But thanks Tony, anyhow.' Anton placed the card next to his phone. As an employer he'd not take kindly to an employee touting for business other than that related to his employers' interests. In fact, the unusualness made him contact his father.

'Just to say I'm near Kings Cross.' These were Anton's first words. He cut to the chase.

'Father, a ticket inspector has offered a taxi service via his brother. To take me to the flat?'

'That's right Anton. It was Izabella's idea. Nice of Izabella to think of you? Don't you Think? Don't worry, be happy. Tony, likes to wear a uniform when he gets an opportunity. He's known as Mr Uniform. Taras, and Izabella, although Brodham residents, maintained associates to contact in the City, should need arise.

# Chapter 10

# Danny's Visit to Linton Farm

'Danny?'

'What?'

'Have the Ledleys gone then?' Asked Alex. They were next to each other on the "A" Frames.

Rural deliveries were a small cluster, set apart from rows of town deliveries. Slots for letters widened due to an increase of packets over letters. Rural delivery post people had rejected the frivol and jingle of Radio One and a light orchestral number was playing on Radio Two - their channel of choice. Rural postal drivers were even known to tune in to Radio Four. Perhaps to be in tune with rural folk who liked to give their views on the Archers and more serious items played on Radio Four. Postal workers with a wide range of both occupational and professional training prior to walking the streets for a living.

Rural Sub-Postmistresses might hold opinions on politicians they liked, disliked or even hated. Vicars, colonels and rural folk in general, not unknown to voice contentious views, perhaps emanating from their interpretation of the "news" behind the news. Danny answered Alex's question about whether the Ledley's had gone with a...

'No, Alex. What made you think that?'

'New owners?' Alex stepped out from his sort frame and held out an A4 brown envelope for Danny to read. It was addressed to a Mr Taras Kedrov, Linton Farm, Brewery Edge Lane, West Frampton. Danny nodded his head.

'They've not left - no, expect he's a tenant. He wasn't going to reveal personal information about the Ledleys to Alex or anyone.

43

'It looks official. I got taken through the back entrance. Don't really know much about them.' Danny stopped there. It wasn't only the confidentiality, that he shared with the Ledley's. Alex's next question revealed another aspect.

'How's Vicky, these days?' was the follow up. 'Back from Uni, isn't she?'

'Don't know,' said Danny, with a shrug of the shoulders, which was a lie. 'I 'spect, so. Don't suppose she'll stay at the Farm.' This wasn't the first time that Alex asked about Vicky but he had no intention of encouraging interest in the Ledley's daughter from Alex. Alex covered his delivery during Easter when he took a week's leave and at a time Vicky was back on the farm.

'I'd take on your delivery tomorrow Danny with a chance to meet up with Vicky at the Ledleys.' Alex's first words to Danny on that previous return from Easter leave.

'She's only there over the holidays. You wouldn't see her normally.' Danny was quick to dampen Alex's enthusiasm. Only too aware of how attractive she was. That the summer holidays were started meant Alex was back to asking questions about Vicky. Their banter was interrupted by a call from Dave, the assistant manager, as he walked by.

'There's a part delivery to cover from three to five. Any takers?' Alex turned around and said.

'I'll do it Dave,' who gave a thumb's up. Dave made to tick a list on his clip board.

'East and North Frampton,' he replied to Alex.

Danny was well into stripping out and banding of post for delivery. Unusually, there were few online packages for 21, Oxton Road. A lighter than usual delivery which for Danny meant more time for his break at the Ledley's.

The lead into Linton Farm was deceptive. A narrow road tarmacked right up to the hedge, which ended by a cattle grid, after a first sharp corner. This lane more than road was made up of rocks, gravel, mud and the occasional dollop of tarmac where attempts had been made to maintain a level surface. John Ledley was strict about a twenty mile an hour limit and blamed the poor surface on post drivers who exceeded that limit. No postal driver could recall a time when the surface was in a good state of repair! Vans were only allowed in the corner of the stable yard, to keep the farm entrance clear. Today, Danny made a point to turn and reverse to the side of the stable door, for a clear view on departure. Lights blinked on and off as he pressed the key fob and walked across to the farm door. Out of politeness, he always, gave three taps on the knocker before he entered.

Vicky, was on her phone, sat at the far end of the kitchen table and pointed toward the green enamel coffee pot on the hob, as he walked across and down the step in to the main kitchen area. On the table, a mug, sugar bowl, spoon and a jar of biscuits with a rubber lined glass top. The glass jar was near to full. When Danny followed Alex, there was never more than a couple of biscuits left. Vicky looked across.

'Hold on, Carol,' she said and lowered her phone.

'Anything for me?' Danny usually left the mail and any packets on the table end, but this time made a pretence to inspect the letters, when he knew full well there were none. A disappointed look toward Vicky followed. Before, he placed on the table, addressed to Mr Taras Kedrov, a large envelope.

Danny walked over to the range. Past experience made him grab the oven gloves from the rail before he gripped the coffee pot's handle. Vicky was back on her phone. Soon he realized that he was a topic of conversation. Laughter, produced dimples in Vicky's cheeks.

How would I know Carol? You can ask him yourself if you like he's just walked in. What's that? Yes, I can ask.' There was a pause. Carol continued talking. Then Vicky said

'Okay, I will, if you like. That's if the answers yes.' Danny, was now sat in the high-backed Chair. There for post visitors and non-family when sat at the kitchen table. Danny, held the coffee mug to his lips and looked quizzically toward Vicky, in anticipation that a question from Carol was about to arrive.

'Carol wants to know if she can re-join tennis at Brodham Leisure centre for the two to four session on Thursday? I said I'd go with Carol, but can't guarantee I'll play.' This sounded good, but Danny didn't want to appear over enthusiastic and opened a Farmer's Weekly on the table, before he said,

'Yes, tell her, yes.' In the male world demonstration of strength, and endurance to impress he was not going to admit that after work, an hour and often more on court, could be challenging with only four players. He'd first met Carol when she was at Brodham's delivery office two Christmas's previously. Danny would like to flatter himself that interest was more from Carol than the other way. That, with male self-affirmation, he was a likely reason for Carol's decision to re-join the postal tennis team. Alex and Scott were possible candidates for attention, but this escaped Danny's consideration. That Carol might want re-join to socialize and for the love of playing tennis and nothing more, could escape his understanding.

A team made up of Alex, Tanya, Scott, himself and now Carol – possibly Vicky? The other three worked with him at Brodham's main delivery office at the entrance to the town's industrial site. Tanya, was an unreliable player, not through her own fault, but because she might work a late shift on Thursday when they regularly met up to play in the summer. Carol would be useful to have there as substitute. Now, that Vicky was to join Carol, Danny's enthusiasm came through and he said, encouragingly,

'Tell Carol, that I miss her at the net to smash Alex's returns from back of court.'

Vicky repeated this to Carol, which resulted in amusement,

probably because Carol said she liked to get her own back for Alex's deliberately sexist remark about her lack of upper body strength. Devastatingly powerful smashes from close to the net to beat Alex were her response.

'She can re-join then Danny?' Continued Vicky and got a "thumbs up."

'Yes, apparently you can re-join the Wimbledon set, Carol. Personally, I think they should pay you, since you're probably the best player.' Danny, was shown a half view of Vicky's tongue, mid -conversation, but talked quickly on.

'I don't know Carol. How would I know? He's just the son of a new tenant that father has taken on to fill barn space between now and harvest time,' Vicky answered enquiries from Carol about Anton. The question about whether she could re-join the tennis group now dealt with.

'No, I probably won't see him. I don't intend staying in this museum, all summer. That could lead to being stuck in the last century with mother and father whilst lined up to look after them in their old age.' Danny wasn't sure, what Vicky meant when she mentioned that about John and Dot Ledley, whom he considered as early middle age, but felt disappointment when Vicky, said she might not be staying at Linton farm. However, this situation moved positively forward with Vicky when she asked

'Are there any vacancies at the Trellis and Vine for the summer?' A pause, at the other, end whilst Carol explained about whether there might be, and other salient information.

'Yes, I can handle George. I'd threaten to tell Suzi. That would shut him up.' Suzi being George's young Thai wife. Danny was given that glimmer of hope that Vicky might stay on if she managed to get summer work at the pub.

'Aunt Kate hasn't said whether the caravan's free for the summer?' Danny didn't get to hear what connection this had to anything. Nor, when the name Gracie was mentioned.

'You do know Gracie? - 'You do Carol. You must remember when she scared Chris Downey.

Grace said that childless married men like him need more experience and technique and followed up with saying her flat had a double bed which seemed wasted.' A pause, followed by,

'Yes, she did!' from Vicky. Danny, made to dip a biscuit in his coffee, but decided against it and took a sip of coffee without dunking the biscuit. Vicky continued,

'Chris went red and turned away to talk to his mate, Dave. Gracie was at Uni, but I never got to know her properly until we met up at the Mayfair.' Carol must have queried where this was.

'You know Carol. Brodham's 's idea of an up-market hair stylist! I'd seen her on campus at Reading, but never knew until recently that she lived in Brodham.' With feigned interest Danny, continued to flick through the Farmer's weekly. Annoyed that Carol wouldn't get off the phone. Out of earshot Vicky whispered

'Man, hungry doesn't do her justice.' Chat would probably have continued, since Carol was quite able to polish glasses and carry on a phone conversation on speaker mode. That was provided that George or Suzi weren't in the bar area.

'Must go Vicky, Suzi's just come back from the kitchen---bye.' Suzi would have gone ape if she knew Carol made personal calls. George could be fooled into the belief that she was into a comparison price check on pubs and restaurants in the area or something similar, but not Suzi.

Vicky replied,

'Bye, Carol.' Danny's, prepared intention to ask Vicky out remained untested, because, John and Dot Ledley arrived back from Brodham. Danny felt, opportunity vanish when the engine from the Land Rover in the yard outside died. He got to his feet. A final drink of coffee dissolved what remained of a custard cream he'd started to crunch.

'You don't have to go just because they've returned.' Vicky's smile reassured more than words.

'Like to stay. but Annette-Miss Hastings will like as not message round to see where I've got to.

'You're sort of under surveillance then?'

'More like a bush telegraph from one village to the next.'

'It's not that Miss Hastings has got more on offer? – like cake, instead of biscuits. Is it?' Vicky knew the West Frampton post mistress back from when she helped out over Christmas. She collected bags of mail to deliver around the village.

'You're joking, of course. No chance that way.' Danny wanted to affirm what he'd heard earlier.

'You might go for a job at the Trellis and Vine then?' Vicky's shoulder shrug didn't really answer his question before her mother walked in.

'Danny, has Vicky given you that letter? And pointed toward the mantel piece.

'No, I thought not. She walked behind her daughter and snatched an envelope from above the clock.

'It's urgent.'

'Not something, usually associated with Linton Farm then,' said Vicky.

'Nor at that university, I would think,' said her father, on arrival. 'We recognize urgency from the seasons. Don't need some electronic bleep to alert us about every second, that's for sure.

Vicky continued to text and ignored her father. Danny sensed that he was an intruder in a family situation. Now on his feet he lifted the chair back under the table. Dot smiled when Danny picked up the letter which she'd put on the table.

'I'll be on my way then. Thanks for the coffee and biscuits Mrs Ledley.'

'I think the stamps are the right amount. Miss Hastings is sure to check.'

'I'll make up any difference, said Danny. 'You can pay me tomorrow.'

'That's sweet of you Dan.' Dot's warm smile contrasted with Vicky's sickly one, when her mother spoke. Vicky was an only daughter, and Danny received attention almost like a son.

'Five minutes. I've just got five – before milking.' John gave the jug a practised shake.

Satisfied that there might be some left grabbed a mug from a tray by the oven. Quiet followed, apart from the repeated clunk made by the pendulum swing of the grandfather clock next to the inglenook.

After Danny's van was heard to start Vicky decided to swing into action with a statement more than question.

'It's alright if I take the Land Rover tonight. To see Carol, father?'

'You'll wanting it as a passion wagon?' he said after finishing his coffee.

'I don't think Vicky has that in mind - Do you dear?' questioned her mother.

'I might. But it would mean the end of any beautiful relationship. It needs fumigating first. Anyway, I'm going to see if there might be some work at the Trellis and Vine.'

'That sounds nice,' said Dot wanting to keep the peace.

'Part time is it?' Asked her father.

'No, I'm going to ask if I can work a twelve hour shift. What do you think?'

# Chapter 11

# Anton Arrives at His Apartment

'Where do you want to go sir?' Steve spoke through a half-opened window.

'Hotel is it?' Sure, enough as Tony said his brother's name was scrolled across the cab window. A for-hire sign conveniently activated on his arrival. Anton felt like saying- "you know exactly where I want to go," as he slung his grip into the back.

'St Pancras Chambers Euston Road, NW.'

'Got you chief, soon be there' said the one purported to be Steve.

Steve and Tony, if that were their real names would be associates and already made aware of where he lived. They might even have been stationed outside his apartment to spy on comings and goings to report back to Taras. Anton wanted his father to be free from the dark underside of Russian mafia connections. Although, no one would want to be spied on by their father, Anton accepted that was how it was and his safe-being was in need of protection.

Visibility in public life required careful planning. There was historically that continuous role play drama run, between public legitimacy and other clandestine activities. There was that conflict of need for protection, whilst he maintained his role of fund manager owner, with need to transmit a level of conformity. He obtained membership of the Kelsey. This followed after Anton secured investments for the director of the golf club.

Situated an hour from central London and solely owned by its members this gave Anton credibility and respect in the right quarters. A Russian family background no hindrance when revealed whilst he mingled with this society level. A change of name was seen as sensible, even helpful for clients. He did not over emphasise family background, but was known to give a polite knowing smile whenever the word oligarch cropped up in conversation. A recent invitation to join a Masonic Lodge was turned down because this conflicted with stated Christian belief, he said. More that religion was used as an excuse to not get involved. Anton already had connections with a brotherhood, which he aimed to leave and was in no hurry to get involved with one more. Enrolment, as sides man and usher at a nearby church was more useful.

Roles requested via St Peter's vicar, after he offered to invest diocesan monies raised from fetes and charity events. Anton would make sure that these gave a better return than conventional market investment. Recommendation and prestige enhancement from the PCC came the vicar's way, because investments made good returns and advice was obtained for free. For Anton it was a good policy. That of involvement with charitable activities.

"Come the revolution," was a quaint expression from the 20th century, but was still valid for a situation where hostility might erupt against wealthy sections of a community.

Anton, might one day need support from vocal members of this church. His father's brotherhood in the past supported C of E, Catholicism, and Islam, wherever there was a distinct concentration and following in town or city. Whichever religion held most influence would invariably be courted. Although he wanted "out," of any connection with his father's activities he valued, at times like this any security it might offer. Anton courted favour with those who might have funds to invest. Kelsley golf club was just about an hour from London, an example. Membership enabled acceptance into the most influential groups, religious or otherwise. A golf club owned by its members with a £60,000 annual membership fee. A good return from member funds was required, as the club's director of finance quickly impressed on Anton. A financial director who was allowed to win conclusively whenever he met up with Anton for a round. A need to find a home for membership funds found Anton centre stage as financial advisor of choice.

Rather cannily, he suggested to the director that his investments made for the church would not be dynamic enough for the golf club. A build up to the mention that the church funds accrued a mouth-watering ten percent per annum return in present economic conditions with opportunity for growth. Reverse psychology in action since church investor clientship added a degree of probity, which might swing a good deal with a business community of influence and affluence.

Lights on the dash board of the cab told Anton that the lights were on, although it was still very much an evening light. Steve's taxi faced Euston Road on the run up to St Pancras Court. He slowed at this point and Anton looked up to the fifth floor and saw that his window's apartments were already lit.

He called, 'Steve, if that's your name, Someone's already in my apartment?' At this point Steve slowed and drew into the side of the road, pressed the hand brake button and stopped the engine, before he turned in reply to Anton's question.

'Steve, is my name for today Mr Kedrov. It's a name you can use.' He neither said Mr Carter nor Anton, although he would be unlikely to use first name terms.

'It is good that we arrived now, because you might not believe me. It will be MI5. You are seeing the under- trade secretary. Is that, not right?

'Yes, but why would they be searching my flat?' Have they suspicions about who I am?'

'It is perhaps a good thing. I have files from computers and

53

a phone in your flat we had to leave but were able to delete anything that might connect you with your father and us, of course. We know exactly what they know about you. It is all good Mr Kedrov. Your tax returns are up to date. You belong to a prestigious golf club. You sometimes even holiday in this country. Cornwall is a favourite location.

'Not,' replied Anton.

'It is from now. I say that it is good thing, because you would not notice that they have been. These people are experts and methodical in their searches.' The lights went off in the apartment.

'I was just thinking,' said Anton. 'There is a cleaner that sometimes works evenings.'

'That might also be so, but it is not this time. We know that the estate agents were approached by the secret service to obtain entry. They said it was routine and, in the interests,

of protecting the area from possible terrorist attacks. We were informed yesterday and needed to fetch you from the train station to show you this and explain how it is.'

'My files and phones?'

'They are in the back of the cab. We would advise that you destroy these.'

'Nice to be back home,' said Anton.

The double doors which led into the apartments opened. Steve opened the glove box and passed a pair of binoculars to Anton.

'Perhaps you would like to take a closer look. He was able to see that there were three of them. One a woman with long fair hair, in a business suit. The other two dark haired with glasses. Both wore brushed jeans and blazers. They would be presumed to be residents.

'That will be a disguise,' said Steve.

'They look typical. They could be residents,' said Anton. Steve pressed a switch in the cab, which lit a sat nav screen, in receipt of a camera response.

'Their car is around the corner, but we set up in the parking area.' The three could be seen on the screen as they entered the car. An interior light enabled a view inside which showed first the woman remove a long fair wig to reveal dark cropped hair. Subsequently, both men were seen to have close cropped hair on the removal of hair pieces.

'It's like a pantomime back stage,' said Anton.

'The word pantomime is not a bad description. I'm pleased you've seen this. You mightn't have believed me if I'd told you the truth'

'You could be right.'

'The Moscow connection?'

'Yes, that was a risk,' said Steve. He delved into the glove compartment and produced several envelopes.

'We removed correspondence from your father with the Moscow valve company. Nothing incriminating, really, but we didn't think that the mention of Moscow was a good idea. I've spoken with Taras about this search. We received a tip off.' A bundle of correspondence was handed back to Anton, who flicked through the letters before stuffing them in an inside coat pocket.

'I'm more concerned about my downloads. More that they are of a personal nature.' Steve then said,

'Don't worry we replaced sensitive lap top and iPad info before they visited. You need to remember that you're an avid Tottenham Hotspur fan and that you are down for a reunion with your rowing club from university days. Also, that we deleted some of your Twitter account and included some verified dates for football and rowing events.

Original files went to a new account. The password and a variation of your email is enclosed here.'

Steve produced an envelope from his inside coat pocket and handed it to Anton.

'That's good of you.'

'You know how it is Mr Kedrov. We always need to be several steps ahead of security forces, but it's really, you know, a good sign that you have been checked out in this way. We would worry more if they did not go to this trouble.' A smile of satisfaction, played momentarily across his face.

'That this country is not rated as a premier player with its armed forces any longer doesn't mean citizens who it regards are useful are not monitored.'

'You're saying that I should be flattered?'

'Not that so much, as that you are more likely to be safe. You can be of use in their schemes. It's good that we've been able to access your details through the coded system set up with your father.

'Very reassuring.' Anton, only informed of this now.

'I will call you a registered taxi. It's someone who regularly visits St Pancras Court and I will drive to the King Charles. Buy a drink at the bar and sit near the door. he will enter and call your name -Mr Carter now, I believe. Is that, not right?'

'Yes. That is my business name.'

The fake taxi scenario was no less a pantomime than that of the security forces techniques. An irony, which was not lost on Anton, who said under his breath.

'When is a taxi not a taxi? - Answer- when my father decides that he needs a fake one.'

'I've your new computer, iPad etc in a case. Before you pay the driver ask him to carry it into the foyer. Stan the commissionaire knows this guy. There will be no suspicion that you know anything about the earlier.

It happened as Steve predicted. There was nothing unusual about Stan's reception, for Anton. Steve proved to be right.

'Joseph. Surprise, surprise. Not seen you in town for a while,' said Stan when he entered with Anton's case. An arrival not unexpected, because Stan, saw the cab driver and Anton on the screen of his bullet-proofed office in the foyer, and heard the buzzer which was positioned in a light strip on the steps up to the St Pancras apartments. Stan, was trained not to reveal security arrangements and liked to feign surprise on the entrance of visitors to the apartments. When he caught Anton, on screen outside behind Joseph, he pressed the door release button and walked out in to the foyer.

'Welcome home Mr Carter. Good journey sir?' This was not wholly a charm offensive on the part of Stan. More, that his health trainer suggested he take advantage of any opportunity to be on his feet. Extra walks, whenever possible, intended to lower weight and hopefully cholesterol level. He moved across to press the call button for the lift whilst Anton paid Joseph. This time a bona fide cab driver, who picked him up from the King Charles. Joseph handed the case to Anton on payment. Steve previously gave Anton a fifty - pound note for the fare.

'That much? He queried.

'Joseph understands the meaning of the colour red. That he's in danger if he talks.'

Anton, now held the lap top bag which contained replacement hard drive and software for machines in the apartment.

'Always good to be back Stan.' He said, but resisted an urge to say "and to see your obsequious smiling face."

'How's the health training going?'

'You know sir it's difficult changing the eating habits of a life time. But thanks for asking. It's you know, how they say-work in progress.' At this point the lift bell pinged and the green "G" light lit up followed with a swish from doors opening.

'Have a good evening sir.'

'I will. I will Stan.' Anton smiled before he turned away to step inside the lift. Until that evening Anton didn't have a determined opinion about Stan, one way or the other. He was employed by the letting agency and his loyalties would be with them. Anton presumed that there would be master keys, but in the tenancy agreement there was a paragraph which stated that tenants would be notified should the owner or their agents wish to enter. With, an explanation for the reason to be given to the tenant within the agreement. Unless, of course there was an emergency situation, like a fire or burst pipe. No mention had been made of an entry by Stan, which meant he might already know more about his business than was desirable and Anton didn't want to stay with the knowledge that the commissionaire was privy to his affairs, even if it was about his legitimate fund company and not about his father's activities. No home or place is quite the same for occupants when it is known that burglars or perhaps that MI5 have snooped around. It was intuitive, but Anton switched the lights and television on and left via a back fire escape to find alternative accommodation for the night at the nearby Burlington Hotel. The case containing his revised life background went with him.

# Chapter 12

# Tennis Interrupted

The score was forty-fifteen when Vicky called back to Danny from the net.

'Hold that serve Danny.' Strains of the Blue Danube floated across from within Vicky's blazer, which hung from a post near the court. After her mother remarked about the previous ring tone she'd settled for something more restful. Tanya was unable to make it and Carol asked Vicky if she could stand in. Danny was now left on court when she left to answer.

'You can't be serious?' said Dan, in despair. He was no McEnroe. 'We've only another point to win the game.'

Vicky held the blazer up to get inside the pocket.

'Yes,' she said and walked across to the grass bank, before she sat down.

'Yes,' she said again. Unsure that there was anyone there. Now confident that none of the others could hear.

'Hello Vicky,' it's Anton.'

'Really? I mean hi, it's good to get your call. I'm in the middle of a tennis game, but it's not that important.'

'I'm due to visit the farm tomorrow to see your father. Finalization of plans.' All of which could've been arranged on the internet or by phone, but there was another reason.

'Would you like to-go out to the Trellis and Vine? It's the pub we discovered on our visit.

It's not exactly the high lights. Do you know where I mean?'

'Yes, it's about the most popular pub in the area at the moment. It's okay, for around here.'

'I know it's a bit short notice. Appreciate there could be

something else on.' He hedged his bets, in case non- acceptance was clothed in an excuse.

'Yes, of course-I mean that'll be okay-in the evening - yes.'

'That's great. I'm due to see your father at about five. I'm sure we'll be finished by seven at the latest.' Vicky looked up to see the racket which belonged to Danny frantically waved at her, before he returned, in a knock up with Tanya and Alex. She smiled at Carol, who was waiting for them to finish, in the hope of getting on court. Vicky broke off from Anton with-

'Got to go. See you tomorrow Anton-bye.'

'It was a music agent.' She said on her return on court. 'There's a second violin part on offer in the Brodham Palace orchestra pit for "The King and I," production coming up.

'Really Vicky?' Called back Tanya - 'Really?' No way was she going to let on that the call was from Anton.

'What's the score?' She called out and retrieved her racket from court side

'It's forty-fifteen and if we don't win this game it'll be your fault, said Danny.

'I don't think so,' said Vicky. 'You've just got to serve an ace, Danny, to get us through.'

Unexpectedly for both of them Danny did.

# Chapter 13

# Taras Instructs Yakov and Oleg

"T. Kedrov Valves-Land and Marine Supplier." A long red lettered sign, with a cream background. Former ship windows were boarded up and a new double door was fitted above the steps which led up from the pavement. Formerly, an angling and outdoor pursuits outlet.

A business that closed after the owner, an enthusiastic mountaineer, fell to his death in the Cairn Gores. His wife, reopened the shop, a week later with a caretaker manager, with a view to sell the lease on. Taras, became the new tenant leaseholder.

Valve User Magazines were spread in wand feature on two glass topped desks. On the back wall of the blue carpeted foyer a model of a Shell tanker in a glass cabinet. Next to it a green painted valve with a red wheel. A printed caption stated- "Valves make Shell go well."

Expanded valve parts, featured on diagrammatic posters, which displayed the intricacies of valve mechanism. Credit needed to be given to Taras, for authenticity, with regard to display and set up, a former Russian trained marine engineer. A white phone sat on a small card table, plus, a visitor's book, with blue wicker cushioned chairs either side. The door to the interior set to the right of the table. Instructions were to dial one hundred.

It was Yakov who sat in the chair nearest the door and dialled.

'Yeah, Taras it's like for real,' He said when the phone was answered by the boss.

'Well, what did you expect? A cardboard cut-out shop front, Yakov?'

'I 've a valve company in Leicestershire which can dispatch valves, by helicopter, to an oil rig, if the customer wants. I'm quite happy with the company, as a bona fide one. It is for me more like a hobby, you see. Is Oleg with you?'

'Yes.'

'I'll release the door. You'll hear a buzz. My office is at the top of the stairs. I will make clear what I want you two to do at the farm when the crates arrive.' A click from the replaced phone. Then, a prolonged buzz from behind the nearby door. Yakov, opened it and they both went up tiled stairs to a landing, and faced gold letters, with "Office," across an opaque door window. Yakov went in, followed by Oleg. Taras, was standing in front of an easel stand which showed Linton farm set midway between a map of southern England, with a map of London, but also the roads leading to Southampton. Oleg not taking any particular notice of the map, exclaimed,

'What do you need all this for?' The floor was set up with four desk stations each with computer screens hidden behind desks canopied on each side by additional screens.

'Because Oleg, this place is for real. I told Anton it would be – this time. Izabella is to supervise a team which will list orders that can be fed into the email system by operators. Izabella understands how to run an office. I'm so lucky that she is good with business and spread sheets. My engineering business will be twinned with the hotel and the guests will have contacts who will assist in promotion in the London Market. This - Taras, tapped the map with a pointer. This is what you need to look at and understand. Here sit at one of these stations and I will explain the journey of the crates from London to Linton Farm. Then from there to Southampton docks.

# Chapter 14

# Anton and Vicky

'What time is that Anton arriving?' Asked Dot.

'And how did you know he was coming?' Asked John who was scraping mud from his boots at the door. He moved forward, but stopped to remove them and stretched across to meet the shiny slabbed floor.

'Vicky went shopping for a dress this morning. I happened to ask when she might be wearing it and it followed on from there.'

'What followed on from what?' asked John as he shoved first one then the other foot into moccasin slippers. Dot, put down a bowl of cake mix and placed her hands on the table.

'That's not the all of it. She said that it's a visit to the Trellis and Vine. To see Carol is it? I asked. But then her phone rang with that, you know, Blue Danube music. I couldn't hear what was said, but the next thing, she said was,

'Anton, says he might be a few minutes late.' I pretended not to follow. Aren't you a bit curious why's he ringing your daughter then? Dot picked up the bowl and began to scoop the contents into the cake tin before she continued.

'It sorts of falls into place then, John. How would you like your daughter married to the son of a Russian, John Ledley?'

'Strapping lad. Be useful round here,' John settled into the armchair.

'Is that all that concerns you? That your daughter's possible future husband might be useful on the farm.'

'Like to see it stay in the family-wouldn't you Dottie?'

'You'd best get out of those clothes and into something more business-like. I've told Luke that I'd help with the milking.' Vicky walked down the stairs with a towel around her head. Her father aware of this, and was in hearing distance when he said,

'I will need to increase the rent for the barns then. They haven't even moved in yet! Well you see, my daughter didn't come with the deal. I think that I'll need to charge extra don't you think?'

'Can't I have a private life? You've told father?'

'Why shouldn't your father know?'

'Let it go, he lives in London. He's likely, got a girl-friend. Perhaps, a wife.' Vicky removed the towel. A cascade of water darkened, hair was released before it was brushed and inspected with a mirror taken from the kitchen cupboard.

'I'd get straight with that one my girl,' said Dot. Vicky knew that mention that he could be married would set her mother off.

'At least I can talk about something other than market prices for livestock or the low pay to farmers for milk from the supermarkets.'

'Very real concerns for your father. What do you think paid for your university course, when you were away.'

Later, white trim on the dress, reached to Vicky's knees. A cardigan remained, in part, unbuttoned to reveal an orange pattern with, blue and yellow flowers. Her father said to Anton at the end of their discussion about barn storage.

'I believe you might be waiting for my daughter?' This was followed by a slight pause from Anton. Vicky was in hearing distance and walked into the front room as he answered.

'Yes, that's right, -if---'

'He's not waiting. I'm ready, you see,' said Vicky now stood next to Anton.

'We're going to the Trellis and Vine, father. Okay?'

'I'll not need to fetch you then, that's a plus.

'Thank you, Mr Ledley. Thank you for settling the conditions of the lease,' said Anton. They shook hands.

'I'll want my daughter back before the lease ends, though.'

'We're only going down the road, don't take any notice Anton.

'Have a good evening, you two,' called Dot.

'We will, Mrs Ledley, we will, said Anton. Outside he led the way to the car. Whilst she fastened the seat belt, asked,

'Is this your car. I mean your personal car?'

'Not exactly. Father has cars for his business and this one's borrowed. I don't drive in London.'

'You're not impressed?' He said. Lowered head feigned, disappointment.

'It's not that, but it just feels like a company car. Not the kind of car that anyone would want to own.'

Anton, smiled.

'It's a Merc, a luxury end car. Cars relate to personalities. Is that what you're trying to say? That, I would need to drive a beat-up Range Rover if I wanted to fit in here. But that's probably not what I would like. It would be a Maserati or Ferrari, although I don't think I'd have time to drive-I get what you're saying.'

'You work for your father then?' She continued as Anton drove at twenty along the farm track.

'No. I act more in the role of instructor and advisor. Even consultant. Help out, when things get a bit technical for the old chap. Will I disappoint you if I said that I'm a fund owner manager.

'Really?'

'Yes, really. It's not how I started out. But I'm my own boss. Maybe, not unlike a farmer. We have good investing times and bad ones. Bit like crops and seasons.'

'Not much.' Vicky, turned back from a look out of the window, and said,

'You're something in the City, then?

65

'Open to interpretation. It's about constant re-evaluation of resource.'

'What types of resource. Is it ethical?'

'Are you that interested! Let's talk about something other than my work.'

'How about an ability to entrance animals with music for them to be more contented.

Produce more milk and crops. Abilities that can mesmerise everything on a farm to growing more productively?'

'That sounds patronizing.'

'It wasn't meant to.' They didn't talk until the Merc turned into the pub car park, and Anton,' said.

'I haven't upset you have I?' But didn't get an immediate reply. They walked toward the porched entrance to the Trellis and Vine,

'No, why do you think that?'

'Because of what I said in the car.'

'Men, assume a woman needs advice. Even when they're not asking. You're, not alone Anton.' He held the door open. Was this going anywhere?

It was Carol's night off. Realization, dawned for Vicky, when greeted by George at the bar with

'Good evening Victoria' which wasn't her name and could be interpreted also as patronizing. George gave Anton a smile reserved for customers who have previously visited and with a valuation for size of bill.

'And welcome back to the Trellis and Vine, Mr Carter. Will you be requiring a? table for two?'

'You remember me George?' I'm impressed.'

'Part of the service, sir. A table for two?' Anton, turned to Vicky and said,

'I've not eaten,'

'You go ahead. I've had something.' She shrugged her shoulders. 'Perhaps a starter'

66

'I'm not an evening eater.'

'That's perfectly okay,' said George. 'We can provide whatever you require from our menu. Young ladies do go for a starter. That's fine.' George picked up two menus from behind the bar and came out to show them an alcove window table.

'This tables not reserved,' if it's all right, for you? or---

'Fine George,' said Anton. An open menu was offered to Vicky and then Anton. This kind of preferred customer treatment was unlikely to continue when she returned to work at the Trellis and Vine.

'Can I get you drinks?' Anton, lowered the menu.

'A lager with lime, Anton,' said Vicky.

'Mine's an orange juice and soda.'

'With ice? Half or pint?'

'Pint George, with ice.'

'Very good, I'll see to that while you decide.'

'You don't drink?' Said Vicky.

'No, it's just not worth the risk.' They'd entered the main bar area and the next bar only came visible to Anton after they sat down. He spotted Oleg, Yakov and partners thorough the beamed opening which divided the two bars. No, he didn't want to be seen to know them. Opportunity arose when Vicky left for the Ladies and he got to his feet only to be met with the George's return with the drinks.

'I'll be back to in a minute.' He said.

'Perfectly in order,' replied George. Anton walked through the oak beamed archway into the more darkly lit bar.

'Anton, Anton, it is good to see you,' said Oleg, as he caught sight.

'She's very attractive,' said Tamara. 'I could wear an orange dress with flowers like

That, but the pink in the hair is a little young for me.'

'Okay,' said Anton. 'I don't want you to make out you know me. Is that understood?'

'You are unkind Anton, said Maya. 'You're ashamed of your Russian friends no?'

'That's not it, at all. I have a private life and anyway it's safer that I'm not seen to be on friendly terms. My father wouldn't want our connection to be advertised to all and sundry.'

'Maybe,' said Yakov. If this is what you wish. We will do that.'

'Melt into the background?'

'She's, returned to your table,' said Tamara. 'Perhaps it will be your lucky night Anton?'

'It's not like that, and you know it.' He walked away.

'Who are they?' Asked Vicky, straightaway when he sat opposite.

'They're visitors for a weekend break. I was curious, because I heard Russian being spoken. They're Muscovites.'

'You can speak Russian. How many other languages?'

'I don't speak Russian that well. I'm better with French and Spanish.' Anton wanted to change the topic and interrupted with,

'Are you staying here for summer?'

'I've no plans, said Vicky. 'But it's so quiet on the farm, unless you like the company of cows, sheep or hens.' Three years away from the farm broadened horizons, but it was where she grew up.

'I like riding, but Cleopatra - that's the horse Izabella went to look at. She's due back, with her foal, next month. I've been asked to exercise her by the owner then, which is great.' George was hovering.

'Yes, we'll order now George.' Anton looked across and Vicky lay the menu down.

'I'll have the pasta-bake starter.'

'And for you sir?'

'Rump steak, mushrooms, chips and peas,'

'And how would you like your steak?'

'Medium to well done.'

'That's fine.' George pressed the screen pad to set up the order.

'And drinks. would you like? Wine perhaps?'

'Not for me. But you go ahead,' Vicky said to Anton. A glass of tap water, perhaps?

'Of course,' said George. 'And for you sir. A little wine, perhaps?'

'No, I'll have the same.'

'Thank you for your orders.' George scooped up the red tasselled black folders, and returned to the bar.

'I play golf. That's when I can get away from work.'

'I'm not interrupting your golf then?' Vicky looked mischievously across.

'Yes, but in a good way.' Anton was attempting to salvage, a not overly successful start to the evening, Unsettled further by a meet up with his father's associates. A couple at the next

table were no longer talking, perhaps, they sensed a more interesting conversation might be about to take place nearby.

'That not how, I wanted it to come across,' said Anton. 'I was worried your father might disapprove. His daughter being asked out by a tenant.'

'Tenant's son, after all.'! Vicky was being mischievous. 'He's not like lord of the manor, Anton.' his name said slowly, tantalizingly as if to say, okay, you've got out of that.

'But are you an enthusiastic golf player?' I consider that a legitimate question from a woman's perspective. A sport known to border on obsessive compulsive with some participants.'

'You think so?'

'Yes, I wouldn't have said so, otherwise would I? George approached with a tray of drinks, which stopped conversation. Anton met his match with responses from Vicky.

Suzi came through from the kitchen door with a tray of

food. A table near the bar had ordered ciabattas.

'The rump steak will be a little longer. You understand,' she said. Anton smiled at Suzi and said.

'That's fine, that's okay. The conversation drifted into talk about university life whilst they ate. Anton concerned that Vicky wasn't impressed with him, but relieved when she smiled and said,

'I'm enjoying tonight. Are you staying in the area? Your father has an office in Brodham high street, doesn't he? Anton's phone pinged, but he didn't respond.

'Don't you need to answer that?

'No, it can ping. When it's important I get a text or mobile message. I should've left it in the car.' He removed it from his pocket to switch it off. Although, Vicky didn't seem to mind, it was another chalk up faux pas. Already. formulated in Anton's mind was a pre- post mortem on how the evening went. Unsure about feelings toward him when she riled at wealth. It was though honesty laid bare, which could be attractive, in itself. This wasn't that kind of date where he couldn't care less if he met the girl again.

That had happened, in London. Accused of being over friendly with the Italian waitress, his date stood up and said

'Anton, I'm leaving.' Only to return and insist that he pay for a taxi, which he did. Whilst, he stayed to finish his meal the waitress came over.

'I hope that the meal is bella I'm so sorry that you are left on your own. But perhaps she was not right for you.' She paused, to remove the place, set opposite and smiled at Anton.

'I'm finishing for the evening. It's none of my business, but I do understand.'

A badge name, with a flow of gold lettering clearly visible, when she leant forward to slightly caress a glass, before it was removed from the table. Opportunity, for Anton to ask, in a quiet voice.

'Petronella would you like to go for a drink?' She, in turn whispered,

'Not in these clothes and I will need a shower, if you don't mind.' To reassure she said.

'It's alright I have a small room in the upstairs. I cannot take you there, though,' and gave a smile, which intimated disappointment.

'I can sit in the bar, and wait.'

'Of course, but we're going somewhere else, yes.'

'Yes. There's the White Hart nearby or somewhere else.'

'No, that's okay. You do not mind. I have no time to prepare my hair?'

'No, no.' Anton, had no problems about the state of her hair, and could see no fault with the secure red ribbon bobbed look as it was. There was though a stunning transformation on Petronella's return. Anton had now moved to a quiet alcove away from the bar. Her fine features portraited in shoulder length luxuriant, even though "unprepared," dark hair. Anton's heart skipped a beat when he saw the transformation. Aftershock from the bad date experience, no longer a problem.

That night she stayed at his apartment, but apart from advanced caresses and kissing there was no more. Intense love-making started a week later. It was Petronella who said that she preferred for this to be everyday but after another fortnight she said,

'I am sad, but also happy.'

'How is that?' Asked Anton.

'Sad, because I enjoy what we have together and that it has to end. But happy because my boyfriend Stefan is tomorrow returning from a visit to his family in Naples.

Anton had already sensed that the intensity of the relationship suggested that it was about sexual chemistry rather than total compatibility and relieved when she said this was the situation. She loved Stefan, apparently, and that they would probably stay as partners and even marry, she told him, but she couldn't manage too well, without regular sex. She hoped that Anton would understand. There wasn't really a choice for Anton.

This date with Vicky he wanted to go well. Why did he allow Petronella intrude into his mind?

Vicky's pasta bake arrived.

'The steak will take a little longer, you understand,' Suzi said.

'That's alright, we understand' Vicky responded smilingly because she felt for Suzi.

'You go ahead,' said Anton.

'No, I can wait. It's piping hot.' Steam rose from the bake and the plate was hot.

In an attempt to enliven the situation, Anton raised his glass and said,

'Here's to a happy holiday.' Vicky went along with this and then asked,

'Why are you not married Anton?' Sample grey threads in his hair. Black hair that can show talismans, more than fair hair toward the march of age. Anton, at least five years older than Vicky juggled a dual role, now that he was involved s with his father's business affairs. Susceptible to a level of stress beyond the average. When he said,

'I haven't found time,' it riled her sufficiently to say,

'That comes across as a chauvinistic remark.'

'No, seriously. It would be unfair for a woman, I mean wife, to be parked somewhere in a London apartment. It's just never been right whilst the business requires high level attention.'

'Am I to interpret from that- that I'm not really getting much attention and that you're just going through the motions then?' This drew a smile.

'No absolutely not Vicky. There've been girls in my life.' Anton quickly adjusted his answer.

'I meant previous relationships. There's no one just now. I'm totally here for you.'

'Woah! That's sweet of you to say, but I don't think. I'd, believe a little boy lost in the big city explanation better.' Anton was unable to reply since George came over and gave a totally unnecessary flick of his serving cloth to remove supposed crumbs before he placed Anton's steak, accompanied with a side dish of chips and peas, in front of him. A decoration of lettuce leaves, sliced tomato and parsley accompanied the plated steak.

# Chapter 15

# Linton Farm

Perhaps, an anomaly, but Linton Farm was of early nineteenth century build. Apart from a front room which overlooked a rockery, the downstairs was open plan. RSJ strengthened; an architect determined that the hall wall needed maintenance for eight feet, plus end pillar support. Behind this walled strip, was an alcove carpeted section with easy chairs, table and flat screen TV.

Dot and Vicky were here, but John Ledley and Luke were at the kitchen table. Luke did have cooking facilities in the studio flat, which came with the job, but he would ask Dot if there were any left - overs from dinner. There usually were. Reluctant to cook, an alternative was a visit to the Ragged Duck for sausage and chips or similar. John attended to numbered returns from the dairy. Luke had managed a follow up mug of tea from the pot, before he said.

'They're watching us all the time Mr Ledley.'

'Who?'

'Those foreman types who supervise the unloading of them crates.

'Much like me then Luke.' John spoke without looking up from the screen. This remark made little impact, but Luke continued.

'No each pallet they want with a fresh label faced outwards and distance measured between each stack going up.'

'You're capable of doing that Luke. You'd rather be doing pallet work than out there in the field all day on the tractor. That's what you said when I mentioned that Jason from Long Farm could come over and do fork lifting. You said you'd rather Jason did that kind of tractor work.

'I know, I know Mr Ledley, but what's in them crates. The crown jewels?'

'Well, I've the shipment notes here from their boss. Mr Taras Kedrov.' John picked the list from the table and read it out.

'Valve wheels, valves, connections and associated infra-structure plus cosmetics. Whatever that means. There's nothing about crown jewels mentioned.' Luke smirked from behind his mug before he drained the remains.

'Didn't think there'd be much call for valves and things round these parts.'

'They're not staying. Due for shipment to Southampton docks it says here.'

'So, I'll be shifting them again?'

'It could be the difference between you going back part time and staying on full- time Luke.'

'Yeah well, I've got repayments on the bike. I need the money.'

'That's all square then,' said John.

'Another thing Mr Led, the gypsies are down Primrose Lane again.'

'Not in the field though with that mound of earth, though are they?' Asked John.

'No just into the grass verge. They've set up with wood carving, like with power saws.'

~

Meanwhile, across in the alcove, Vicky flicked from channel to channel before she pressed the off switch.

'Switch it back on to the farming programme,' said her mother. 'I like to watch that. It makes farm life look to be rewarding and straightforward. You don't get to see long hours and the back-break side of real life.' Vicky switched the TV back on, found the channel and handed the remote to Dot, who, immediately turned the sound down. It was about the housing crisis in farm areas.

'Depressing that is, but how did your evening go then?' Vicky stopped texting and sipped her tea in a display of nonchalance

'Okay, I suppose. Don't think he's my type. Bit too serious. He's a fund manager, would you believe?'

'He might be keen to buy the farm. They invest in things, don't they?' Dot was wedded to the farm but always made out she'd missed out on life as a farmer's wife. Vicky, pulled a face.

'Father wouldn't want that to happen,' anyway, it's not going anywhere.

'Just asking, that's all.'

'Is that Carol you're texting? You are still keen to get a job at the Trellis and Vine? That's Before you do something with that degree?'

'I haven't got a degree until the dissertation is accepted. Jobs in music aren't that easy to get. I might if the worse comes to the worst have to teach.'

'Nothing wrong with that,' said Dot.

# Chapter 16

# Police Visit

Dot was cooking the breakfast a month later in September when John said,

'I've sold the remaining potatoes to Andy Phillips.

'The fruit and veg man at Brodham Market?'

'Yep.' A conversation interrupted with a shout of,

'Those boots come off outside the door-not on the way in Luke!'

'Forgot, Mrs Ledley, just forgot.' He hobbled with one boot in hand to place it away from the floor which was now muddied, and walked across to sit in the chair, which looked across the farmyard.

'They say, Mr Ledley that my bike's worth more than I paid for it at the dealers.'

'That seems unlikely Luke?' John fielded Luke's often naïve view about business and the world in general from his arm chair at the head of the table.

'The replacement model isn't rated as any good. Jack says mine's like an investment could sell five like it in a day. That's what he said.'

'Probably said that to get you to buy another. Keep you interested, Luke. Crafty, really. There you go, telling me, about this, but my biking days are probably over.'

'They are John Ledley,' said Dot. 'They are as far as I'm concerned.' Toward the end of breakfast Luke, enquired.

'Not sure whether I've had a second mug of tea, Mrs Ledley?'

'Pass it here then.' A swish of tyres led Luke to stand up to get a better view of the farm yard.

'One of them unmarked police cars have just arrived.'

'How would you be knowing that?' Asked Dot, as she passed him back a refill.

Luke pointed toward the window.

'You see, that's' Constable Barry. I know him. He drinks at the Ragged Duck. It's quite a lot quieter when he's there. Mrs Beveridge, behind the bar said that he quietens things down. She said that when I asked why it was- like gloomy one night. Then she points him out to me. That's how I know Mrs Led. They chase speedos on the motorways, in cars like that. Bit sneaky, though. They-pretends to be like a rich git in a top motor. Then those blue lights flash from end to end, before they pull someone over to the hard shoulder.'

'I hope they're not after you Luke. Get on and finish that tea.'

'I don't want to meet with them, anyhow.' Luke picked up his mug, gulped it down and was out the door before there was a rat a tat from the Ledley's police callers? Dot turned to John, who was now sat in the inglenook on his iPhone to access spread sheet milk yields from the dairy.

'You've not reported anything about farm theft have you John? I mean recently.

'No, there's those jerry cans that went missing, but I was wanting to get rid of them anyhow. Dot went to open the door.

'Chief Inspector Perkins, Brodham CID. This is detective Constable Barry.' The Chief Inspector was in a dark blue suit and allowed a smile to flicker in and out of the introduction.

He raised his hand toward Constable Barry. Now, conveniently arrived by his side. Shorter than the constable with receding black grey hair, the Chief Inspector reached out.

'Mrs Ledley?' Dot hand shake response. An automatic reaction to that direct approach, where politeness needs a response.

'Yes, what do you want Chief Inspector. Do you want to speak with my husband?'

An identity warrant was momentarily produced by the Chief Inspector, but there was little doubt that they were the genuine article. Perhaps there was an astonished look on Dot's face.

Previous attempts to get a visit after farm theft delayed and looked into only much later. after forms were filled in online.

'We've just finished a late breakfast. You'll have to take us as you find us. John was now stood up by the inglenook and put his iPhone down when they entered the kitchen area.

'Mr Ledley, apologies for this interruption, but we're investigating some unfortunate incidents that we believe occurred yesterday evening. The Chief Inspector shook John's hand and continued with,

'I'd like to speak with both of you, if that's all right. I enquired with a Miss Annette Hastings at the West Frampton post office, if you're wondering how I already know your names, you do understand.' An explanation which accompanied a satisfied smile.

'Yes,' said John and directed them to the settee in front of the inglenook. He sat opposite Dot in the arm chair.

'Fire away Chief Inspector when you're ready.'

'Might I ask, is there anyone else living with you?

'My, daughter.'

'Vicky's at the Trellis and Vine Chief Inspector. It's a holiday Job, said Dot. And there's our farm hand Luke Harker. He's put up in the studio flat above the converted old barn,' said Dot before John could answer.

'I'll get straight to the point, if I may,' said the inspector. We believe that you might perhaps unwittingly be storing illegal substances in your barns. Customs intercepted crates at Southampton docks on transit to China. There were valve parts which contained quantities of illegal substances. We have information that valves stored in your barns are identical to those that were intercepted at the docks.'

'Well Chief Inspector this is news to me. We advertise storage space through our agents. Perhaps they're the people you need to see. We accept tenants in good faith.'

'Quite. But I have to remind you that HM Customs have wide ranging powers and they might need to inspect items you have stored.'

'Raid us. Do you mean?' Asked Dot.

'I wouldn't like to use terms like that, Mrs Ledley. Customs officials, like ourselves.' The Chief Inspector included Constable Barry with a glance in his direction, 'are only going about their lawful business for the protection of the wider community.'

'Right Chief Inspector. What are we supposed to do in the meantime?'

'Nothing. That's why we've made this visit. I'd be obliged if you make no mention of this to your tenant. A Mr Taras Kedrov, we understand. Further investigations are to be made.'

'This isn't a wild goose chase is it Chef Inspector?'

'Not at all Mr Ledley. We're here to pursue all avenues of enquiry. Our visit is purely to appraise yourselves.' A polite smile, included Dot in this appraisal, 'of a possible visit from HM Customs.'

'Only possible?' Said John.

'That's all I can say.'

'Might I ask where the illegal substances were bound for?'

'Not at liberty to divulge Mr Ledley. I'm might say just a messenger.'

'Messenger for whom?' enquired Dot. There was a nod of the head.

'This incident has international implications and I cannot tell you more. Nor should you let this information go beyond this meeting.'

# Chapter 17

'It was Suzi,' said Carol. 'Not George, when I went to the kitchen. She just said we have a customer's friend who returns to work for us, but she is not to have special privileges. I asked who it was – and she said it was you – like as if we'd never met? You know what she's really saying, don't you? It's more that she believes every woman who works at the Trellis is gagging to get George into bed. When it's more about fighting him off!' Vicky smiled back at Carol, before she placed a dried glass on the tray and picked another.

'Anyhow how was it for you Vicky. Going out with a boss's son.'

'Anton's independent. He only helps his father. He's a fund manager.'

'A fun manager?'

'I didn't say that.'

'I know, but I could do with one of those. A fund manager sounds good, though. You could give up bar work.'

'Bar work is not my life's destiny – I hope. I'm happy that Annette wants me to exercise

Cleopatra three times a week. Pays good for just three hours daily work. Better than what George and Suzi

pay. Problem is Cleopatra's up for sale. Don't know how long she'll want me.' Vicky returned another glass to the tray.

'This job's temporary for the rest of the summer and the world of finance doesn't interest me either.'

'I could get interested in a man in that world.'

'You're just saying that. What makes you think that I wouldn't marry for love?'

'Are you seeing him again?'

'Maybe. He's near my age and not bad looking.' Carol gawped at what she considered an understatement. Vicky wasn't giving any more away.

'He's going back to London. I'm not bothered either way.' Vicky decided to leave Carol guessing.

'It's my early night tonight.

'And it's your day off tomorrow.'

'Yep. I'm playing tennis. I'll see you Friday. I'll give your love to Danny when he asks after you.'

'You won't.'

'What's wrong with Danny?'

'Nothing wrong with Danny. Only that he's like - a bit of farm machinery. That he happens to be the postman, who occasionally works on the farm. Mother would adopt him if she could.'

'Then if we got together it would be like incest.'

'It wouldn't Vicky. How'd you make that out?'

'Don't you dare stir it Carol. Anyway, if you think he's that fit why get me involved – don't, for heaven's sake tell him that I'm interested.'

'Alright keep your hair on. I won't.' Vicky phoned her father for a lift. Walked to the corridor at the back of the bar to fetch her coat. But returned to wave a finger at Carol with a final reprimand of

'Don't.'

Two locals were sat at the bar plus a husband and wife, at a nearby table when Carol heard George answer the phone in the kitchen. A decision that the couple were husband and wife, made on the basis that they sat in silence. Apart from an occasional splutter from green logs ablaze in the fireplace and a murmur of voices it was quiet before George called out from the kitchen door.

'There two guests to stay overnight. Call me when they arrive will you Carol?'

'Man, woman, alien?' Carol, liked to disturb George's precocious mine host manner, when Suzi wasn't visible.

'Two gentlemen who happen to be Russian. They stayed before and were delighted with the service, food and overall hospitality.' George didn't suffer from false modesty.

'I remember them as a bit brash, but they didn't throw their glasses in the fireplace.'

'They're paying guests who buy more than a single pint. I'll have you know.' A nearby bar stool patron rattled his paper, but said nothing.'

'Okay, I'll watch out for them, George.'

'They'll need, Carol, to sign the guest register under the bar. Alright?'

'Yes, I'll see to it George, don't you worry.' Suzi. Perhaps should have seen to guests on first arrival, but wasn't overly keen on front of house.

# Chapter 18

# Oleg and Yakov Return from the N.E.C.

'I never want to go again and now we are told only to speak English by Taras!'

'Do you think that was Anton?' asked Yakov.

'Who else? And Taras he says the Brits will not trust us if we speak Russian, together. Never mind that, I do not trust myself when I speak English! Did you think it wise, Yakov, to give that bar woman the website address for Izabella's cosmetics business at New Street

'Why not? Rail train stations are good places to meet potential customers. She will talk with her friends. It's legitimate business. We will not attract attention.

'Yes, yes. It suits that there is movement into cities like Birmingham, and London. Cups and saucers rattled as a refreshment trolley arrived at the end of their compartment.

'She is very pretty. Do you not think.' Yakov turned to Oleg 'Yes, to you and me Oleg,' but Rashad, you know the Arab, who always has a hot racing tip, said that he was interested in white educated young women, preferably under twenty-five, to buy for employer. That hostess is probably under twenty-five. Ten years ago, they would give £50,000 pounds, but now they want women who have degrees and higher education. British education over here can give them a taste for young women with similar education. A slave needs to be more than just a trophy. It is a match they want, even the wealthy ones. Love, perhaps of a different kind.'

'Love of a young white woman's flesh and love of wealth for the woman can match up.'

'No, Yakov, you are so very cynical to think this. But what

surprised me was when Rashad told me that in each region young women are on like a shopping list. He said that he has now an agency. Look.' He handed his iPad over. Across the top were the words "North West" beneath six photos of young women illuminated the screen."

'Whenever the woman is identified and located, he will receive payment to a middle eastern bank. It is straightforward in that all clients must own private jets to take the young women out of the country. Rashad has specialist kidnappers to capture a target woman. Some they are attracted, anyway. But there needs to be an intermediary who can work with the group to make everything appear normal. The woman is made to sign a contract of employment before she leaves and will have a passport. Even if the authorities are able to find her, she will by then be too frightened to say that she didn't agree.' Yakov scrolled down several pages which went through north east, central, south east and then he said,

'Ah, I have reached the south west region, where we are situated.'

'Is there anyone we know in these photos?' asked Oleg. There was a pause then -

'That's unlikely – but, a minute, yes, there is. Look!' Yakov, held up the iPad with a photo of a young woman who was stood by a horse. Details underneath read that the photo was from Horse and Hound with the caption "Vicky and Cleopatra at Linton farm." When Yakov zoomed in he had little doubt that this was the young woman who was out with Anton at the Trellis and Vine. He swiped clear, as the hostess trolley arrived. Yakov, flipped the cover over the iPad and placed it on the table.

'Coffee for you two?' The drinks hostess smiled at Oleg, who was nearest.

'Yes, we would like coffee Abby,' replied Oleg. Her name badge, was dark blue. Name in silver. He produced first class tickets, which gave entitlement to free coffee, but she said.

'I don't need to see any tickets. White? Black? With sugar. Perhaps biscuits.'

'Black with two sugars. We've had a busy time at the N.E.C. This will help to keep us awake.' He said this more to Yakov, than the girl who she set out cups and pored the coffee, afterwards, the train gathered speed as it cleared a tunnel. Yakov waited until the hostess was busy with passengers further along the train and said,

'Rashad needs an intermediary?'

'Yes, but how much will be paid to the intermediary for location with access to the woman.?'

'There's a code for each region. One moment,' said Yakov. 'Rashad gave me a card.' Yakov removed his wallet and flipped through a bunch of cards.

'This is it.' He read out an entry - SW 54383X. 'Here take the card,' and handed it to Yakov, who had re-opened the iPad cover. After the code was entered the photo flipped over to reveal a printed statement-

"Intermediary payment for location assistance of £500,000, paid in £100,000 instalments. One of two final payments will be made when the jet leaves the UK, A final one when merchandise is delivered to the client." Group designated for acquisition will give requirement details.

'Rashad, he says that the client is a prince.

'So, you already know about this!'

'I did not say that I knew this woman. I just said do you have you pictures for this region. I was astonished like you when I first saw the picture. I pretended not to know who she was and asked if there were other pictures.

'Rashad first showed this photo where she was dressed in riding clothes and held a whip no, no, Oleg, it was not like that. The pictures are of attractive women, who might be seeking a man.'

'Or woman?'

'Yes, maybe, that. But she was dressed like a real horse woman. The photo was taken from the magazine, as well. With the coat and tight fitted ride clothes, you know like they wear the skinny jeans, and again she was by that horse. I then asked "Why is there this special customer interest?" and he said.

'That, young woman was at university with Prince Aza and he will pay a very good price to whoever can get her.' I said

'That means that he's obsessed with her.'

'Yes, that is so,' he said, 'but he has the financial means to buy her as a slave.

I said it looked to be very lucrative and he gave me this list of the young women who are sought by the very wealthy.

'But then it's not the business we are in, Yakov.'

'Izabella would be interested though,' he said, 'Do you not think?'

'Maybe, she will say that now she is legitimate and has no need of extra.'

'I know Izabella better than you. It would be too good an offer for her to resist.'

'But, how can this young woman be taken by the group?'

'Perhaps, with the interest she has with horses something can be arranged. That is the role of the intermediary. Rashad, went on to say that he's now able to pay the same standard money for attractive dark- haired as for fair-haired blue-eyed women. Arab princes have preferred female white slaves to have fair- hair and blue eyes. He said that they can be under thirty, not as before, restricted to only young women less than twenty-five years.'

This market has much expanded, Oleg, from a few years ago. I believe that Izabella will be tempted.

'Times have moved on. I sometimes think we would be better able to sell young women to the Arabs than drugs to the Chinese, when we go the Engineering Conference.'

'Are you going to suggest that to Taras?'

'No, he would disapprove, in the way that the Arabs disapprove of drugs and alcohol.'

'You, think Izabella could do this without Taras knowing.'

'It's worth a try, do you not think?'

Oleg and Yakov, were previously, supposedly at the Advanced Engineering Exhibition to assist Taras's office employees with advice to customers, but in turn, to trawl the show for cocaine contracts. The display products on selected Chinese stands exhibited identical or near identical valve and pipes, to those they exhibited. It just meant a switch of exhibits in the evening when the public had left the exhibition centre. Each of Taras's valves contained street cocaine to the value of a quarter of million pounds. Payment to one of Anton's trading account in Switzerland, avoided the launder complications of those through the British system. Chinese cities with an upwardly mobile middle class were supplied with cocaine via the Bahamas.

Taras had tapped into this lucrative market when cruise ships stopped at Southampton on passage from the islands. A conference centre became a useful venue to sell cocaine, but also, a source of further networking for other outlets. Oleg and Yakov initially returned to Brodham to report back to Taras, on the sale of ten caches of cocaine. Display equipment and exhibits for the show were previously taken by lorry from the warehouses to the NEC. This delivery consisted of two pallets and plinths for product display, plus company leaflets, four touch screen display units, tables, chair and a hot - drinks machine. Stand and tent were in the price of the registration and booking fee. Valves and pipes exchanged at the conference with the Chinese, would be returned to the warehouse at Linton Farm. For this conference Oleg and Yakov stayed at the Holiday Inn and left Birmingham New Street at eight twenty-seven, Saturday morning. Taras, said that it was better that they blended in. They would have preferred to have the blend in higher up, at a five-star hotel, but Izabella, more than Taras insisted this would look bad in front of their two female employees.

# Chapter 19

# Police Visit Bella & Patrick

'Tebbet's Farm's, different Josie.'

'Different in what way?' They were leaving the station for Primrose Lane, police officers Josie and Bill. There'd been a break at Linton Farm. Stolen crates taken from farm buildings were to be returned to Taras, which calmed Izabella. Her work force saw no change, but Taras would be less harassed. Josie and Bill were on a follow up investigation. Plain clothes were directed, that theft of these crates and boxes was to be considered low key. Unworthy of much expenditure in either resource or time.

'It's different.'

How's it different?'

'They're travellers aren't they Bill? Josie, inspected eyeliner in the mirror of the visor, but never applied make up once in the patrol car. No, she wasn't interested in Bill, but station knowledge said that Janice was. Janice, now sergeant level, did little to disguise her interest, and Josie was not in the market for upturning that relationship. When out with Kevin Pitcher, on alternate shifts, it was different. A firm believer in equal status for male and female officer, though Josie felt that Kevin wouldn't notice overmuch or remark if he saw her stripped topless in the passenger seat. He did become animated when he was asked about Rol, his Retriever. Name shortened from Revolver. Josie, accepted that women were incidental to his life, rather than of particular interest. Josie, now wanted to know more about the inhabitants of Primrose Lane, and not to further her relationship with Bill. A black four by four close on fifty, slowed to forty when aware that a police car was behind.

'I take it you've never visited Tebbet's Farm with the bailiffs?'

'No, but who'd want a brick through the windscreen.'

'Know about that Jos? - That incident, then? They're known to vamoose to Scotland for twelve months to avoid an electricity bill. No, this visit is nothing like that - one occupant family in Primrose Lane. It's not a static caravan site, like Tebbet's. Well, semi-static, I should perhaps say. Dead give-away, when the address Primrose Lane was given. We're just on a visiting to let them know that we know they've handled stolen goods.

'No brick through the windscreen?'

'Unlikely,' Bill smiled across at Josie before they turned off the main road from Brodham to join a minor road, which led to Primrose Lane. On arrival they stopped at the beginning of the layby. All that could be heard was the swish of wipers. A caravan with a lean to was up on the verge next to the hedge field. A four by four parked in the gap next to a gate, but not blocking it. A thin smoke wisp broke apart above hedge level from a pipe chimney at the far end of the caravan.

'Someone's at home by the look of it. D' you want to go and knock on the door? Perhaps

they'll be more receptive to you Josie?'

'My being a woman, as against a man? I could have you for sex discrimination, Bill Stanton.' Bill's brow wrinkled, but she unclipped the seatbelt and reached up with both hands to smooth down her hair, in preparation to wear the uniform cap once outside, before softening her stance.

'No, I see where you're coming from. Perhaps, I should accept that as a compliment. That we women have softer skills, as against males who charge in all guns blazing.' She didn't wait for a reply.

'I'll knock on the door. But you can be outside those closed window curtains.' Josie pointed to yellowed laced net curtains. With phone in one hand Josie lifted and tapped the caravan's knocker three times. As predicted, there was a twitch from a curtain. Travellers response could be abrupt and aggressive when court proceedings for ordered departure were in place. But, also had that ambiguous relationship with police, when it was, they who needed protection. A woman's voice called out

'It's the Fuzz Patrick. What you been up to?' A deep voice belied the age of a young woman, who opened the door? Hair tied back in a clump. A pink smock reached to just below waist level for house cleaning. Right hand glove was removed to open the door. Not long out of her teens, but not a mother, Bella, was Patrick's latest partner. His brother and wife would join the two of them later. Josie pretended not to have heard the previous call that Bella made to Patrick.

'I'm police constable Josie White. We're here-that's officer Bill Stanton.' Bill removed his cap as he approached the caravan door.'

'To make enquiries.' Bella's frowned face lit with a smile. Perhaps to win sympathy, at least from the male officer, if that should be required, in connection with Patrick.

'Are you on your own?

'No, I'm with Patrick.'

'What's happened?' There were previous happenings in Bella's booked events that might warrant police visiting. Bill took over the questioning.

'And you are?'

'Bella, Bella Morris. We're here to help at Linton Farm. That's all.'

'Not quite all. May we come in?' Bella turned and called out.

'Patrick, you'd best come here.' There was a thump of feet on the floor of the caravan and Patrick's stockinged feet appeared next to Bella's rabbit fur slippers.

'What's it you want now?'

'Just a chat about some crates.'

'I got them fair and square from some European gents. Paid for them I did. You'd best see them-not me.'

'We will, in due course, but we need to track their movement.'

'You're not here to take Pat in then?' Said Bella.

'No, no it's not like that.'

'You'd best come in then.' Bella's house work had not been in vain. Patrick never noticed either way, but one of the police was a woman, who might be particular about how the caravan was. Three-quarter way down from an open door away from the kitchen and toilet shower facility, an unmade bed could be seen on one side behind curtains. The other one, Bella's returned to a day sofa. Bill placed his cap on the dining table. Bella pulled back chairs. Patrick slipped behind the table followed by Bella, whilst the two police sat down opposite.

'Right, the traders paid you one hundred pounds for six crates and there was at least five hundred pounds worth of cosmetics and toiletries in total.

'I didn't know that did I. They took a fancy to a bear that I'd carved.'

'Patrick learnt sculpture and art at college. People don't always have cash to pay,' said Bella. 'I've told Pat that you don't know always where things come from.'

'They wore suits, drove a Range Rover Discovery. The crates were towed in a trailer.

Them sort of people don't always have ready cash and I knew the contents is sort of what sells at a market stall.'

'You don't remember the registration number do you Patrick?' Asked Josie.

'It was red. I do remember that.' Said Bella. 'they said that the bear would bring them luck. They had that way of speaking that made you think they were-

    'Russian, perhaps?' said Josie.

    'I suppose so.

# Chapter 20

# Izabella – the Boss

'Yes, Izabella, they are holding the crates. The police have said that forensics will need to look at them, but that afterwards we can have them back.'

'It is because you are Russian Taras and it is discrimination, because of the perfume bottle and Novichok. You do see that, don't you?' said Izabella.

'Maybe, maybe not.' It's complicated. The gypsies in the lane were found with the crates after a trader at the market was suspicious about where the cosmetics came from. I don't know what more they know.'

'Five of my crates have been taken from the third warehouse. Why was not that Mr Ledley? Reporting this to the police and us?

'Because they sawed through the padlock on the outside and replaced it to make it look okay.

'Wasn't the door locked?'

'No, and that must have been Oleg or Yakov who didn't lock it. It could have been worse.' There was a knock on the office door.

'Yes,' called out Taras. The door opened

'Mr Kedrov.' It was sales input assistant Natasha.

'What shall I do with the listings for the goods that are still at the warehouse that are with the police? Earlier Izabella made it known that certain items would no longer be available.

'Natasha,' It was Izabella who replied. She picked up an inventory from Taras's desk and handed it to her.

'These are the goods affected. You will need to put all the holdings to "not available." I might not list them here anyway.'

Natasha looked towards the desk. Although, Izabella was her boss she would have preferred it to be Taras. From whom she received a faint half smile.

'Do what Izabella says, Natasha. When the door closed, Izabella sat in the middle of the three arm chairs in front of Taras's desk and got his attention by saying,

'One good thing is that I met up with Annetta from the post office.'

'Why is that so good cherie?' His screen, a picture which showed storage layout inside the barns. He knew that the only part that lacked CTV coverage was the rear of the third barn.

'You're not listening Taras,' said Izabella. Taras put the iPad on the desk and placed his elbows on the desk to appear attentive. It was that difference of fifteen years which ensured Izabella could when she insisted make Taras give her, his undivided attention.

'Of course! I do want to know why it is good that you met up with Annetta, cherie, of course?'

'We met at Latin Dance class.'

'You never told me that you were going to Latin Dance.'

'No, because you wouldn't come and for a Russian you are poor dancer. You have two left feet.' This didn't appear to upset Taras.

'No, no don't get me wrong, Izabella. It's mixing with local people. That is a good thing.'

'So, but Annette, Miss Hastings she is smart. Like Americans say a smart cookie. In one bedroom she has photographic studio. My range is outside of Amazon and she can photograph for online sales. My cosmetics range is special and will need good photos. I will pay her five per cent for each sale.'

'You do not pay her anything else?'

'I have the brochure Taras.' Izabella opened the red handbag and produced a catalogue

'I shall have this and I believe she is right when she says they are quality products. Online they will sell for a little less and be attractive to customers. Except, Taras that they are with the police!' Expediency of the moment favoured Taras when Greensleeves started playing on his smart phone. In the company of Brits, he would say, "I so love this old English song, you know."

'Yes, it is Taras Kedrov speaking.' A pause followed.

'No, no, sergeant it is no bother. It is not inconvenient. You say that the crates have been looked at, Yes. I can send a van to collect them before four o'clock. That is very helpful. Thank you for calling. Yes, I understand it is procedure, yes, yes, quite alright, goodbye.' "The gods have been favourable to me," he said. More to himself than Izabella.

'We can have the crates back. Is that so?'

'Yes, the police have released your cosmetics.'

'I should think so. They had no business to hold them. It's good. I will be able to contact Annette. Izabella, leant forward, and raised herself from the armchair. Taras' smile was activated by view of shapely thighs, revealed when she knelt to pick up a handbag, but also, in part, relief from the near return of the cosmetics crates.

'I will see you this evening. I am busy in the main office, Taras.'

'I understand cherie. I am so pleased for you.' Taras didn't see pursed lips when she turned to leave. A low-level murmur from the main office switched off the moment Izabella reached the outer office. She announced,

'Before first lunch break, I will see Eva and then Martina.' Izabella, looked towards her work station.

Eva, put her work on save and sleep before she walked after Izabella.

'Close the door.' Eva closed the door. Izabella, positioned, against the front of her desk facing forward, hands

98

outstretched on its glass top.

'You have been twice late this week. A second time means you forfeit twenty pounds from your pay. Yes?'

'It won't happen again Izabella.'

'But it has, yes? Twice, is again. But you are young. Nineteen years I see from your application.

'Have you boyfriend?'

'Not at the moment. I am too busy for that.'

'Perhaps, later then. But you share with Martina. I have to see Martina. She is like you, but only once is she late. I do not want this to continue. I will give Martina a warning, but perhaps you would not like to pay this fine.'

'Money is needed for the rent. We pay alternate months. This month it is my turn Izabella.'

Izabella walked across and turned the key in the door.

'I can offer punishment instead,' she said and walked back to open the drawer of her desk. She withdrew a long triangular metal ruler.

'I ask if you have boyfriend. Martina is not like your partner?'

'No, we are not like that.

'That is good. There might be little marks, you understand.'

Izabella, moved from behind the desk and leant forward.

'It is three on here and you have paid the fine.' Her hand gently squeezed Eva's right cheek beneath the jeans pocket.

'You understand?' Open-mouthed, Eva blushed, said nothing and looked submissively downwards.

'Turn around, lean forward-more, more - elbows on desk. Here put these in your mouth.' Izabella grabbed a clump of tissues from a box on the desk. Eva took hold of them and did as she said. Almost immediately the triangular ruler made contact. A stifled yelp came from Eva and then another and another.

'There, that is all.' Izabella placed the ruler on the desk, before she reached forward to lift and caress Eva's hair.

'It is over now. It was not too bad for you, no. You can stand up.' There were tears trickling down Eva's cheeks after she removed tissues from her mouth.

'It is not easy for me to do this, but you have said that the money is important. Here take this.' She gave Eva a fresh tissue to wipe her eyes.

'There is cream for pain relief out of my new range. You can be first to try it and then give a good review comment afterwards, yes?

'Of course, Izabella.'

'Loosen your belt turn around again. Pull down your jeans.' Izabella, opened a display cabinet and removed a tube of cream.

'Now, lean forward for me once more.'

Eva did as she was told. Three red stripes could be seen either side. Connected criss-crossed lines visible when Izabella lowered Eva's briefs.

'Oh, it stings,' her face grimaced momentarily. Izabella, applied the cream with a caressing motion of her hand.

'There it is over now. I cannot promise this alternative if you are late again,' she adjusted Eva's briefs, who stood and turned to face her attacker and boss.

'You will not be late twice again, no? Do not tell anyone. You understand. It is just between you and me. You're okay, no?' Eva moved away from the desk.

'Yes Izabella. I do not lose any money from my wage?' Eva, turned away and zipped her jeans.

'Yes, you are good girl, no? You can pay the rent, and now fetch Martina, yes? But say nothing to Martina or anyone. There can be no opportunities to model if you do tell anyone. I do not want to lose either of you. Okay?'

'Yes, Izabella. Thank you.'

Izabella walked across to unlock the office door, whilst

Eva re-tied the belt around her jeans. A smile of satisfaction remained on Izabella's face when Eva returned to the main office.

# Chapter 21

# Report Back for Oleg and Yakov

That afternoon Oleg and Yakov were in the lobby of Taras's Engineering outlet. They knocked, to be let in to the main office. They caused Natasha to blush and interrupted the gathering before Taras entered with a sheaf of invoices to be sent online. Consignments of cocaine, but sold as valves at the NEC. Invoice numbers were crucial. Those which began with a P and ended with an X described cocaine sales as against normal engineering sales. There was relief that stolen crates were released by the police, but now Oleg and Yakov were back from the N.E.C.

Taras, had sent them for a closer inspection. John Ledley was initially apologetic, when on the phone to Taras, but he was pleased to learn that the crates contained cosmetics for online sale by Izabella. This was about to change with the return of Oleg and Yakov.

'Boss, boss,' called out Oleg. 'We need to speak.' Taras waved his hand for them to follow him through his door, opposite to Izabella's. He walked across and stood behind the desk.

'Shut the door. What is it? Sit down. What have you to tell me?' Just as they sat in the armchairs on front of the desk Oleg blurted out,

'It's PX257 to 263 they're missing.'

'Are you sure?

'Yes,' said Yakov. 'It's further into the barn. There's a gap. I have the plan.' He removed two layout plans from his jacket pocket, opened the first, and pointed to a text box red square in the racking.

'Look, there they are. And now.' He stood up and placed the first layout on the desk in front of Taras. Alongside, the layout as it was now, which showed a blank space.

'It looks like they knew that there was no CTV. It's likely a rival in the market, Taras.'

'Not the gypsies, then?'

'We don't think so. The cosmetics crates were marked with their contents. Whoever took these knew what they were looking for,' said Oleg.

'Were you followed back on the train, last week? Did you talk about the work?' A euphemism employed for illegal cocaine smuggling. When gold was in transit to another country the term used was recycled material or just RM. Understood acronyms.

'No, Taras, we never mention the work, ever, it is not something we would do.'

'The padlock was replaced. We had to saw through to gain entrance. Our key would not fit.

'It is clever, because Ledley would just pull at the padlock, if he checked.'

'Yes, why would he want to go in. And then until the police traced Izabella's cases of cosmetics no one knew.

'We think Taras that, whoever went in was watching. Probably not the gypsies, who ended up with Izabella's cosmetics. It would appear to be planned and not just a break in. Taras had located PX257 to 263 on his screen inventory list.

'That is good.'

'What is? Asked Yakov.

'They are returns from the Chinese. They were not as clever as they thought Oleg. It is unlikely whoever took these two crates wanted them for practical use as valve machinery.

We were just lucky. But I believe they might have taken the cosmetics to make it look like that was what they were interested. It also has appeared like that to the police.'

'It wasn't travellers then,' said Yakov.

'Maybe, but I think it unlikely. It is no great worry, at the moment,' said Taras.

'I need the lease lorry firm to be ready to move crates to the docks next week. There should be no problem with the authorities and now Anton tells me he is to speak with the Transport secretary next week. It is good to be connected with government.

Funds can enter my account ready for transferral over to Anton's to finance the government's new parking scheme.'

'How is it that you are needed to supply the British government with funds to build their own projects? Asked Oleg.

'Because they cannot raise taxes without causing new unrest and there has been a clamp down on Russian oligarch investment in London. It's simple. With this connection we will not be under suspicion. Anton's fund is helping the state and that means we can be safe. And maybe, they just like me because I'm Russian, who knows?' Taras, smiled.

'We Russians are like a spare bank that they can turn to when the population is not spending enough in the shops to tax.' He said this to reassure himself as much as to answer Oleg's question. His explanation interrupted by the lilt of Greensleeves.

'One moment.' It was Izabella.

'Hi, cherie...Yes, they are free to see you. I will send them across now.' Then a pause.

'Yes, a van has been sent to fetch your cosmetics. You knew I would do that, straightaway.' A pause.

'Yes, the utmost urgency. Bye cherie.' He turned to Oleg and Yakov.

'Izabella would like to see you. I've finished now.' He returned to viewing the screen on his desk while they got up and left to visit Izabella. Taras dwelt on the consideration that he needed to remake the story. Taras could see a point where Oleg and Yakov might become risky to have around. Anton would understand that they were part of his old life. An accident could be planned. A holiday reward where they were together on a plane, perhaps. It would be tidier for Tamara and Maya to be with them. Taras, would inform the Russian president of their deaths and how distressed he was, but also that they might not have been totally loyal. He had no plans to return, but nevertheless, recently secured a contract with the Russian Navy to supply valves. A safety net for possible future favours.

That there could be evidence arranged to implicate Taras and Yakov with the British authorities, would play well with his need to be seen to be loyal to the President. Early dealings with Russian police convinced him that they liked open and shut cases. Better from their point of view when persons, can look plausible as wrong doers, regardless of any evidence. That Oleg and Yakov could be seen to be enemies of both states, could be a desirable situation.

# Chapter 22

## Intermediary Role for Izabella

'What news have you for me? I asked for you to look at business opportunities,

Oleg?' Asked Izabella.

'You've received instructions from Taras, about the barns and the future transit of goods. Have you anything of interest for me?' Izabella, was of the same view as Taras that it was better that they were now cooperating with government security forces, than on the outside, and under closer surveillance. This reminded her of ambiguities so commonplace in Russia. That making money could be both easier and safer when the state needed your services. Income from drug traffic and illicit sales could be bundled into state payments, which would be seen as permitted and waved through as clean money within a British bank. Neatly sheltered under that umbrella called national security.

'Extra contracts will be good for business. It ensures that you can be paid and it's all legal. But at the NEC what other possibilities were there,' asked Izabella.

'You know Izabella this was an engineering show not a beauty parlour exhibition'

'Yes, but you talked with that Rashad, the Arab. Don't tell me that his bosses have lost interest in suitable young white women?'

'No, no more than those gang bosses who want them for "call girl," work, said Yakov.

'Izabella,' he continued, 'we were understanding that you no longer want involvement with that business.'

'What business is that Yakov?'

106

'That of introducing young women to wealthy persons. A beautiful people agent, rather than a property agent, you used to tell us that you were.'

'It depends, I could be persuaded by price.' Yakov smiled at Oleg, whilst Izabella became excited, about an order on screen.

'Six, six cosmetic boxes from a shop in Bond Street. That is just the kind of order I like.'

'There, there, business is doing really well then,' said Yakov.

'But, don't let on that you are Russian, that's all,' Oleg added, jokingly.

'Yes, but with all these overheads, like office workers. And not all are sales like that one. A cash injection could be useful.' Izabella picked up her sales catalogue.

'We did make an interesting discovery,' said Oleg.

'Really, and what was that?'

'Yakov give me your iPad for a moment' on opening it he scrolled down.

'Here, Izabella, look at this.' He thrust the iPad toward Izabella - recognize this young woman?' Izabella, lowered her catalogue. Interest aroused when she saw a photo of Vicky stood holding the reins of Cleopatra. She recognized both horse and rider, but said nothing save,

'So!'

'That young woman is the one in the Trellis and Vine with Anton.' said Oleg.

'So! She could've had a photo taken for Horse and Hound, that country magazine. They have in doctor's surgeries here, estate agents. What's so special, about that?'

'Because Izabella she is wanted? A young woman that Rashad said Prince Azad would like to acquire.'

'That's fanciful. I mean how much is he prepared to pay?' It was Yakov, who then said in a matter of fact way.

Fifty thousand - pound payments, up to a final payment

of a quarter of a million pounds. Oleg liked what he heard. How Yakov negotiated a reduced price for Izabella. That the intermediary, Izabella, would get half the offer price.

'That's on delivery to East Midlands airport. A final payment when the jet, with the woman aboard arrives in Saudi Arabia. A total of two hundred and fifty thousand pounds.' Izabella's catalogue nearly fell from her hands, but she recovered and continued to flick through the pages.

'I would have to arrange the capture then?'

'No. That's the reason we said, this would be something you would like. There's a group that Rashad employs for the abduction event. But they need local support so that the young woman is seen as temporarily missed rather than abducted. A situation which appears safe. Long enough for a vehicle to take her to the airport. Papers and a passport will be prepared. This young woman would be just another on police files, unaccounted for.'

'It would need enticement so that she could be snatched and quickly taken away,' said Oleg.

'Let me look at that photo again.' Oleg, retrieved the photo.

'Give it to me for my large screen.' Oleg sat down in a nearby chair and sent an attachment to Izabella. The picture gave better definition of both Vicky and the horse.

'I do recognize this horse. It belongs to someone I know.' Izabella didn't say who, but the white flash across the horse's head identified it straightaway as the horse which belonged to Annette. Izabella, knew that Annette only wanted to keep the foal and had seen Vicky exercise Cleopatra. A plan was developing. Perhaps she could persuade Annette to place a for sale advert in Horse and Hound. Also, she would praise Vicky to Annette. How well she looked after the horse at Linton, whilst stabled there for Annette. Yes, there were possibilities.

'You have details from Rashad?'

# Chapter 23

# Meeting with Junior Minister

Anton, could see a positive future. Provided, that he secured a contract with the Department of Transport. This would mean further legitimate recognition for his Fund with endorsement by government, plus, a Saudi Arabian contract through the British Embassy meant under the wire deals by his father, could soon be ended, hopefully.

A tinted window Range Rover, from the company's stable was selected to visit the junior minister at Heron Tower. Anton would be accompanied by Carin Hanson, who assisted with preparation and tying up of loose ends. Dual roles. Personal Assistant and chauffeur. Carin retained ambition to enter Formula one racing. Although not akin to the sport now liked to be in her chauffeur role, rather than just in PA appointment to the boss. A Range Rover was a stretch away from Formula one, but it was an opportunity to be away from more mundane matters. That she wore a chauffeur's cap, like a drill sergeant, who drove a highly ranked military person was not what Anton envisioned, but he valued Carin's eyes and ears when she removed chauffeur cap and transferred to PA role. This chauffeur position happened after Henry retired. His role was as much handyman and goffer as that of chauffeur to the boss. Carin's female colleagues made a fuss of our 'enry, and staged an office party with poppers, balloons, cakes and crackers. Henry moist - eyed said that he'd miss everyone. It was the next day when Carin finalized plans for a directors meeting with Anton, that she said,

'Mr Carter you'll need a new chauffeur, when I travel with you to meetings. I can't do the handy man side of it, but I've contacted a reliable guy from check-a-trade for that part of Henry's role. I can set it all up, if you're agreeable?' Carin possessed that PA skill where pre-plan usually meant fait accompli. A boss then manoeuvred into agreement, almost immediately.

'I've no objection to that. If you're happy Carin and it's not impinging on your PA role. But I can't pay Henry's salary,' Anton was about to leave for golf and in agreeable mood.

'I've thought about that Mr Carter. I visit my dad once a week. That's on a Saturday and I like driving, but there's no point in owning a car. Company cars don't go anywhere at the weekend' Anton was sending a message to his golf club, but replied,

'And, you would like the loan of a car? Yes, that's okay, but you'll need to sort personal insurance and I'd like the same petrol in the car on its return?' he replied. Exactly the answer Carin was hoping for.

'That's really good of you Mr Carter.' Later on, a crossover belted jacket and cap were chosen, organized by Carin. When she obtained approval for the pre-selected cap and top, Anton said

'Quite happy with a match of trousers Carin, if you want. Go with the cap and top.'

'I'd prefer to wear a skirt when driving a luxury car Mr Carter, if that's okay with you. I can put the cap away and transfer to a PA role more effectively.' Anton was not going to disagree. Apart, from leg appeal from a man's perspective Carin's personality was softened when she wore a skirt. Previous trips were mainly to company investment directors. It was Carin who suggested Heron Tower as a meeting place after she noted that Zircon National Distribution had acquired investment in the building. A message to the concierge, led to her being able to reserve an apartment for the Department of Transport's junior minister. Research revealed that the minister was from ordinary origin and not Eton educated. Unaccustomed to lavish living, but likely to be in awe of a penthouse suite. His entourage given the apartment from Tuesday to Friday. This gave opportunity to prepare for Anton's meeting on Thursday. It was not sufficiently high powered to require attendance by the Minister for Transport. Carin deduced this to be the vibe back when she first arranged it. Anton, unknown to Carin received a mobile number from his father to contact associates on arrival. Disguised as a cleaning firm who were visibly at work on the floor of the penthouse suite selected. Carin checked that the pent house was in the name of Zircon Distribution, with no mention of government connections. It was probable that security deemed this necessary, and she was able to talk the under manager into escorting the two of them to this south penthouse suite. When they stepped from the lift into the corridor which led to the apartment, two capped male cleaners were machine buffing an already highly polished floor. Only Anton noticed the tap of the cap. Carin counted seven, eight nine on the doors before they arrived at number ten. The under manager knocked discretely on the door occupied by the Junior minister and entourage. Outside the door numbered ten she whispered,

'That could be wishful thinking.' Anton's appointment was for eleven. A woman, in a navy trouser suit, opened the door. Looked past the under manager, who stepped to one side.

'Is that Mr Carter?' The door opened into a hallway.

'I'm Jane Albright, secretary to Tom Draycot.' Carin did the introductions

'Mr Anton Carter and Carin Hanson. I'm PA to Mr Carter.'

'Good to meet you sir. Tom has been so looking forward to see you – please follow me won't you?' A polished oak door led into a dining space. There was a shuffle of papers as they entered. Tom Draycot, junior minister walked from the head

111

of a long dining table requisitioned for their meeting.

'So, pleased to meet you Mr Carter. At last we meet. Spot on time. A smile in Carin's direction.

'Carin's my PA. Here to take notes and see that I ask the right questions and give the right answers.' Tom Draycot shook hands with Carin and held Anton's momentarily longer, before he responded with,

'Might I call you Anton. Everyone seems to know me as Tom.'

'Fine by me,' replied Anton. His secretary drew back two chairs next to the head of the table and opposite a floor to ceiling window. Before she sat down next to Anton, Carin said.

'What a fabulous view. Might I have a look?' A question directed more to Anton. There were silver mounted binoculars in the alcove window which overlooked the City. Tom Draycot replied.

'Of course. It would be a shame to visit without having a look.' A civil servant's raised eyebrows caused glasses to fall down her nose. Six places were filled with government officials, but the contract was already prepared to cover all eventualities by lawyers and accountants from each side. Forty per cent government funding, against sixty per cent from Zircon. Departmental view was that with Anton's responsibility for private investment, they could reliably expect a dividend return. State intimation that monies raised would then be returned to local authorities to get them on side.

Tom Draycot, led Carin over to where the white binoculars were on a raised plinth and adjusted their angle

'There, that takes in the main landmarks,' and drew back to allow her, a view. He then called out,

'Daphne, our guests would probably like a coffee. Would you be so kind?' A much younger woman than the civil servant with glasses stood up and smiled at Anton.

'That would be great,' replied Anton, relieved that Carin was working her charm with Tom Draycot.

'I would like black with one sugar. Carin, white coffee without sugar- thanks.' He smiled across at Daphne, who left to make the coffee. A door opened to a kitchen on the right. Another similar door was to the left of this penthouse dining room.

By the time Carin returned, from viewing the panoramic view, Anton was skimming through contract papers, already set out on the table. Everything moved forward a pace. Tom Draycot was a keen golfer and conversation drifted into the merits and demerits of particular golf clubs. Carin, meanwhile accessed facsimile documents electronically, to ensure Anton was signed up to the correct agreement. Anton previously yellow highlighted crucial paragraphs. A shoe nudge under the table startled Anton. She dutifully smiled and said,

'Okay. They're okay.' In all the process lasted no more than twenty minutes before documents were finalised and signed by both parties.

'Very good to meet with you Anton and the lovely Carin,' said Tom Draycot. Carin feigned a grateful smile. Yet again his remarks elicited a look of disapproval from the glass wearing civil servant.

'Must dash. They want me in the house for a crucial bill to allow the ban of diesal in all town and city centres. It won't go through this time, but it'll move the debate along.' This appeared to be a signal for most to leave, bar Jane Albright and three others.

'Mr Carter,' Jane Albright looked up from an iPad that was angled in front on the table. 'There are other department officials who would like to speak with you. Carin may stay here with us. As she spoke the door to the left opened. A tall, shaven headed man in a blue suit, which failed to hide a muscular frame stood with hand outstretched.

'Can you please step this way Mr Carter. I cannot reveal more at present.'

'They have clearance from the Department, it's alright Mr Carter. She gave a half-smile and turned to Carin,

'Would you like another coffee? Mr Carter will be a little while.' Carin appeared to be startled.

'Don't go anywhere. I won't be long,' said Anton, to reassure her and walked toward the door.

# Chapter 24

# Change of Circumstance

This next area, a spacious sitting – room could have displayed further panoramic view from floor to ceiling, but near closed venetian style blinds prevented this. Strips of sunlight danced across walls and into Anton's face. It was not until he was several paces inside that he could see that the far side of the room was occupied with computers on desks. Two operators wore ear phones. Two women together on a two-seater were seated opposite three others. Two grey suited men in look out position either side of the main windows. Hand movement by one toward his inside jacket pocket, didn't make Anton feel that this was a check on a mobile phone or wallet. Five others were seated across settees, fronted by small tables littered with coffee cartons. A blazer and jeans guy flicked through a sports channel on the wall mounted TV. In front of an electric fire with arms behind his back stood a tall upright figure who Anton surmised, although in a dark suit would be equally at home in military uniform.

'Name's Julian Reynolds. Do take a seat Mr Carter. We're allocated to industrial national security by the government. Ministers and politicians come and go but you might say we remain to help keep the ship on course.' The words "deep state," formed in Anton's mind. This Reynolds person pointed across to five blue wicker chairs, positioned, away from the others. Anton seated himself in a chair which kept the window security detail in view. Reynolds sat opposite.

'What do you want and why do I warrant this reception?'

'Good questions and I will answer them Anton. Might I call you Anton?'

'Does it matter? You no doubt hold information about who I am. You could address me by file reference number if you so wanted. I imagine there is one?'

'We want to work with you and your father in a mutually beneficial way both for your family and HM government. We are just workers in the field. There is no reason for us not to be on amicable terms, is there?'

'I'll leave my response on file, if you don't mind Julian.' Those who raided his apartment might well be in this room.

'That's alright.' Julian Reynolds, if that's who he was, gave a half smile, and raised a hand.

'Alison, load the footage, to view on main screen, will you?'

'From the NEC do you mean Julian?'

'Yep, for starters.' Julian stepped forward and turned to look at the screen on the wall above. Seconds later a split picture appeared, which showed overhead video, now stilled, of two stalls. Anton recognized his father's valve company display stall, but was unfamiliar with the other one, which was manned by Asian sales people.

'Let it run now Alison,' said Julian. A camera homed in to Taras's company stall and focused to pick out braised insignia markings, cut into light blue valve pipes. This was superimposed on to the main picture. Below identification number and letters could be seen 497158 VTZ.

'You recognize this product and this is your father's exhibition stall, yes?' Without familiarity with the product it might have presented a problem, but he recognized Oleg at the side of the stall talking to a customer.

'Appears to be. But what's unusual about that. There's a trade show every summer?'

Anton, at this point realized that this exhibition and his father's company had been part of a covert investigation by this internal security branch.

'Yes, but I will return to the second stall – a day later.

116

Alison bring up the next picture, will you?' Immediately, a similar picture appeared, but this time for the Asian stall. A camera zoom in picked out the identical valve on display. Same insignia clear to see. Anton had an explanation.

'Perhaps, they bought from father's stall to sell themselves. It's not unknown for companies to re-stock when they need to meet customer requirements, rather than leave a disappointed customer. What nationality are they?'

'Main land China, but okay, you have a point Anton. But the situation became of more particular interest to us – Alison, the close - up evidence photo.' A stripped - down photo of the valve, again, with insignia in view, displayed a small mound of white powder by the valve and visible within the piping.

'Unusual,' said Anton.

'Unusual, unusual. You must know what this is?' Julian went to the screen and pointed at the small mound of powder.

'Why, should I?' Anton prepared to distance himself from knowledge of the illicit drug trade as long, as possible.

'That valve, which came via your father's stall was opened by customers on our instructions after a raid on containers at Southampton docks. Containers bound for Saudi Arabia and finally, China. How can you say that you have no knowledge of this cocaine trade? We can trace back further. These valves were stored in a barn at a farm. We followed the movement from Holland where the valves were made and we believe first loaded with cocaine.' Alison, came in with,

'I have a photo of the farm entrance. It's called Linton Farm.'

'Thanks for that Alison. Yes, Linton Farm. And I understand your father has the lease of three barns?' It didn't look good. Anton was about to say that he would like his solicitor present, when events took an unexpected turn.

'We know so much you see Anton, but there is British state interest with, you might say, events in China and also Saudi

117

Arabia. We do not have evidence of your father selling into the home market. He would be wise not to. You can see that we know much, but authority has been given from the highest level to allow consignments to slip into the Chinese market. In concurrence with security policy. Western intellectual property has been and is under cyber threat attack. Cocaine and illegal chemical drug supply, at present is not technically disapproved of. That is to main land China. Middle and senior management level addiction to cocaine usage is viewed as a retaliatory policy. Addiction, useful to western interest at both macro, economic and political levels.

We would need an understanding that no sales of cocaine were made in the UK, should your father be prepared to assist. We would also consider an over-look of past activities, provided that your father is prepared to offer us assistance?' Anton wanted to know more.

'Where does Saudi Arabia come in all this? In fact, how does father's trade with China impact elsewhere?'

'Good question. That's a good question. The bottom line is that once your father's transport system was accessed it became apparent that firstly it was way off grid, which is great for us.

That's the situation at Linton Farm with the barn storage. Plus, that he has a defined truck fleet access to and from Southampton docks need has arisen for transport to dispatch five containers of gold bullion to Saudi Arabia to facilitate MOD oil replenishment of underground storage facility. The MOD don't want international state eyes to be made aware that this transaction has occurred. It is expedient to buy with gold.

'In the interests of National security?' Asked Anton

'But of course, exactly that.' Anton didn't ask further questions. He didn't want to delve deeper into the whys and wherefores of this international deal. That contract which he'd just signed was probably put in place to spring this deal, in the first place. Anton wanted to secure his father's position. He needed to do some explaining that might help.

'I can see that we are useful to one another. My father and his partner Izabella run in turn a legitimate marine Valve and engineering company and online cosmetics supply company. But he was coerced into the supply of cocaine by the Chinese at an earlier trade fair and forced to continue.' This was an on the hoof fabrication by Anton, but now that the Chinese were exposed as a threat to national security, his story might carry weight going forward. Julian continued.

'You understand. We understand, that your father is a qualified marine engineer and also that he felt threatened by the Chinese a few years ago. It was likely difficult for them to understand that they could have had the protection of the metropolitan police. Your father has interest in the City. But, yes, then we also realize that Russian state police experiences might've held him and Izabella back from coming forward.' This all sounded good to Anton.

'His trucks we see handle more legitimate goods than illegal.' Anton took his opportunity to make a point.

'Obviously, I would like to see an end to father's involvement with illegal trade, myself.'

'But not quite yet you see Anton. Anton leant forward in his chair and asked.

'Are you-your department- going to approach him about this deal?'

'No, we believe you can do this. You do see your father?' Anton was bemused at this question. Why did they bother to ask? All of his movements would've been monitored.

'We've a secure number which can be contacted. It's best that you and your father cooperate do you not think? I'm sure you can see this to be in both you, Taras's and Izabella's best interests.' A look away and then – 'I can rely on your support then?'

'Yes. I'll explain this to my father,' Anton replied. There was no other choice.

Right Mr Carter or do you prefer Kedrov. Here's the secure number. Julian showed Anton an iPad which displayed - 22776069.

'Here.' He held out a pen and yellow post - it pads.

'Write it down. You'll I believe be able to remember. It's not a difficult selection?

'Yes,' said Anton.

'When you are comfortable in your mind to have remembered it please tear the note into four, before you leave.' This Anton did almost immediately.

'We're ready to leave.' Carin was in the midst of a download from the Department of Transport.

'Just two minutes. I'm nearly there with this.' On catching sight of the brown folder Anton held under his arm, she pointed towards it.

'Do you want me to look after that?'

'No, no, Carin I'm needing to look at it. I'll have a coffee, though there's no hurry.' He revised his readiness to depart and decided not to appear agitated. Walked across the room to select a sachet for the machine that the department presumably had installed. He was unsure how much knowledge was shared, if any, between separate arms of government, but decided that a relaxed style was probably appropriate. He selected Americano. Fingers tapped noiselessly, whilst he waited for the process to complete its pour and added two capsules of milk, before he placed the paper cup on the table and sat opposite Carin. It was near to a whisper when he said,

'How'd you like a weekend in the country?'

'Separate rooms?' replied Carin loudly enough for a nearby civil servant to deduce that there could be an implied inappropriate relationship. Then Carin did say it, to elicit such a response. A provocation with words to those in the room.

'But, of course,' Anton smile, suggested that there would've been a different response were they in private.

'I've to visit Linton Farm. In connection with my father's business. Are you frightened of farm animals?' Carin's nod and wrinkled nose preceded by

'Of course not. That's the four legged as against some two-legged ones.'

'That could be taken that you don't like country folk,' said Anton.'

'That's untrue. Quite the opposite,' she replied.

'There's some explaining to do.' Anton sipped his coffee, looked across to where civil servants were either texting or like Carin were at work on a lap top.

'I'll explain some more when we're back in the car-okay?'

'Yes. Do you mean tonight-afterwards? I'll need to get back to my flat first.'

'We can stop at that Italian place nearby for a meal. That's if your boy- friend won't mind, that you're eating with the boss?'

'No, it's his turn to cook. He'll be happy if I say that he can have a take away, because I'm away on business. I'll message before I log off, if that's alright Anton.'

'Go ahead. I'm just going to say good bye to the Grande dame over there.' Anton, got up to walk over to where Jane Albright, the senior Civil servant in charge of proceedings was sitting. She dismissed an assistant when he arrived and smiled toward Anton as he approached. Anton, unsure about how much she knew about the second meeting with the security services just said,

'That concludes the finalization of the agreement, preparatory to the signing?'

'Yes, Mr Carter. No doubt, your financial director and legal department will need to go through the contract documents, but you can be sure that once signed you will receive full government funding. It's been good to meet you.' The hand he shook reminded him of the neck of a dead conger eel when picked out of a boat. Both cold and limp.

# Chapter 25

# Carin Receives a Call

Carol read the occupation of "personal assistant," in the visitor's book at the Trellis and Vine, which was how Carin signed in.

'You're a real Personal Assistant?' Carol looked at Carin, almost as if she'd discovered an alternative life form, that she'd only read about. Although, she'd travelled further afield on foreign holidays and to nearby towns, other than Brodham, the title of Personal Assistant, she associated more with that of experts in a celebrity world, certainly distant from the Trellis and Vine.

'Yes. We have single rooms booked I believe?' Carin answered, without bothering with an explanation. George, came across from the where he'd greeted Anton.

'Good evening, I'm George, so pleased to have you stay here with us. Mr Carter, is a very welcome visitor. Suzie, that's my wife has prepared bedrooms four and five, Miss Hanson. Mr Carter has informed me that you're here with him on business, concerning his father.'

'Yes, that's right. Can you show me to my room please?' Carin smiled wearily. Today's work had been longer than anticipated.

'Mr Carter has double - bed room number five and Miss Hanson single number four Carol, perhaps you'd be so good as to assist Miss Hanson with the two cases.' Anton had carried these in. Carin's was medium size to his smaller one, which was always packed and in a Range Rover, for sudden overnight stays. Carol, came out from behind the bar and fetched the cases from the entrance. On her return Carin said,

'It's okay, I'll carry my own suitcase. It'll make it easier.'

Carol was pleased for a release from regulars who believed that she was interested in their lives beyond serving drinks and being sociable. That they were her parents age and older gave limited shared interest.

Anton, was now able to call his father from the privacy of an alcove away from George and the main bar, and made to look out of the window, whilst his call rang through.

'Bad news, yes you've been rumbled.' Anton was not going to mince his words, but he wanted to get his father's attention to a worried level before he revealed the escape plan.

'Obviously can't talk about it now, but there's a way out, provided you go legit in the UK.

That's all I can say.' There was a pause,

'Carin's with me. We're staying at the Trellis tonight. I'll be over tomorrow. You're settled into above the shop premises in Brodham?' Another pause, whilst Taras revealed some news about his mother.

'How is she?' You want me to visit her? She's asked to see me?' Anton's mother had been sectioned and was still in a secure ward. Anton, never made outright accusation, but blamed Izabella.' This was perhaps unfair. Alisa, Taras's first wife and mother to Anton suffered from a bipolar condition, which was masked from him for some years whilst he was at boarding school. Then, Taras was found to lack application in the for better or worse part of the marriage. Anton's mother had antecedents who came from Russia after an escape from the 1917 revolution. But she grew up as an English woman. Taras who was probably more in line with Izabella culturally than his first wife.

Alisa, with high cheekbones and magnificent black tresses of hair, but now like Taras's mixed with white strands. Bright blue eyes when lit by a smile gave insight to once great beauty. Physical attractiveness is not in itself protection from attacks of mental disorder, but could help a patient obtain kinder treatment before age digs in claws to remove youthful physical appeal. Alisa, saddened to lose Taras, maintained Anton's affection.

'Tell mother to expect me,' he said to Taras, before he ended the call. Carin, would have preferred a suite bathroom to shower room, but she felt refreshed when she sat down on the bed in a dressing robe, whilst the dryers warm air percolated between her hair. An evening meal was booked for eight. It was seven thirty when her secure phone made a swished sound like wind through a beech grove. This was unexpected. There was a text message.

'Be prepared to be shut out from talks between Anton and his father. Need to know whereabouts of Oleg and Yakov? Can you sleep in his bed?'

'Whose bed?' Carin texted back.

'Anton Carter or Kedrov, of course. Give some reason about being scared sleeping in the country. That you're frightened on your own. He's a good boss. You've said that you're with Simon. He's unlikely to make advances, is he? And whatever you do don't allow it to go further. Understand?'

Carin wasn't sure that she wanted to believe that Anton necessarily wouldn't make advances. An owl tweet pierced the silence through the partly open window.

'Okay, I'll go for it. I mean make an excuse that I'm scared to sleep on my own.'

This was additional to her main task to gain the trust of both Taras and Anton. With Anton she felt confident that he had no suspicions that she worked for the security services. Carin, had still to meet his father. Izabella with form, with sale of slave sex sales out of eastern Europe and into Arab countries, but apart from Taras's recent activity through NEC trade centre deals with the Chinese there was no record of Izabella's present involvement in slave trade activity. Information, about both Taras and Izabella were committed to memory. For all intents and purposes Taras ran a bona fide engineering business out of Brodham, which specialized in the provision of marine equipment.

Carin felt a twinge of disappointment, when she arrived at their table. They were alone in a separate dining room, but there was barely a glance from Anton towards her, although she considered a change from suit to red and blue patterned skirt, with white blouse and scarf, might achieve a response. Carin, however, was accustomed to quiet spaces, in the role of PA, when Anton texted or made to talk on his smart phone to the London office. Simon would have been told off if he remained quiet and didn't make conversation, but Simon was boyfriend, and in this inside placement, Anton was technically her boss. Eventually Anton switched his phone off.

'That's it for today.' Carin tried not to make a response that looked like relief. A first course had arrived at the table when Carin said.

'Your father must have a large work force to run?'

'Not that large. There's an automated packing system, which labels and prepares dispatches.'

'Quite high-tech then?'

'You need to be these days. There's a couple of guys in the field. I don't have much to do with father's business. Carin knew this to be untrue, but she smiled.

'Are they British. I mean local?'

'No, they're from father's home town. They're responsible for warehousing. There's just a shop manager and a couple of staff. Is there anything else you want to know?' Carin sensed that she'd progressed far enough with this line of enquiry, but felt that the two Russian were most likely Oleg and Yakov.

'No, just due diligence, in my role of PA.' A dismissive shrug of shoulders and smile helped defuse ideas that she was seeking information and not just making polite conversation.

'Like that skirt you're wearing.' Anton, actually responded, but this compliment probably standard response to any number of women.

'It makes a statement in here.'

'The right sort, I hope?' said Carin.

'Of course, you've got George scurrying around.'

'George? You mean the waiter?

'He's also the Landlord.'

'Oh, does that mean we don't have to leave a tip.'

'That's one way of looking at it. Not, probably the one George would want, though.' Anton paused.

'Carin?'

'Yes,' she said, but the conversation ended on George's approach.

'I've brought over the sweet board, should you require sweets.'

'I'm all right.' Said Carin, 'but don't let that stop you,' she looked across toward Anton.

'No, I'm fine. I'd like a black coffee. Do you??'

'Yes, but make mine white, please George.'

'Certainly sir, madam.' He placed a small blackboard on an adjacent table.

'Feel free to order sweets, if any entice, won't you.'

After George left with their plates, Carin picked up on Anton's earlier remark.

'You were asking me about something or were about to?' George was out of earshot before she spoke.

'I've arranged to visit my father and Izabella tomorrow morning after breakfast.'

'Izabella?' Carin needed an element of surprise, to protect her cover.

'Izabella, is father's latest partner. More business, I feel on her part than romantic, you might say.' The coffees arrived. George fussed about adding the milk to Carin's coffee and felt unable to continue until he left.

'But your mother Anton, where is she?' Carin's researchers located an older sister who now lived in Britain, after a broken marriage. Also, the whereabouts of Anton's mother was known to Carin, but she needed to claim ignorance.

'I know it's probably a bit out of your job specification, but I've arranged to visit my mother tomorrow afternoon. She believes I should be married.'

'But I have a boyfriend and....

'Yes, I mean, that's why, I mean you're not a family member. That means she'll be more amenable, more subdued.'

'You sound like you're talking about some wild animal. Where is she?'

'Alsa, my mother, is in the secure unit at Brampton's psychiatric hospital.'

'Right,' said Carin. 'Then she's sectioned?'

'Afraid so.' Carin feigned unawareness.

'It must be difficult for you.' Ability to withstand emotional involvement with case personnel was tested. There was no time to contact HQ. A decision was needed.

'We're to visit your father and his partner Izabella tomorrow morning, aren't we?'

'Might need to go for a drink after visiting a psychiatric hospital. Perhaps, the boss could give the chauffeur the evening off from driving.'

'Yep, okay I'm happy to drive there and back. Perhaps, we can have a drink back here afterwards. I also find those sorts of places scary.'

'Thanks Carin, appreciate your coming along. Out of the line of duty.'

'Anton, perhaps I could ask a favour?'

'What's that?'

I'm scared of owls and... and you have a double bed. I know it's a big ask, but could I share it with you. I don't think I snore and with a good night's sleep,'

'With a good night's sleep, you'll be better equipped for a visit to see my mother.'

'That's true. Now you put it like that.'

'I've one or two business matters at the London office to message about. I was planning to turn in fairly soon.'

'Okay, if you just give me a call at number four – next door.'

Anton, tapped on Carin's bedroom door in his dressing gown at about ten past ten.

'Not too early for you is it?' He said when she opened the door.

'No not too early. I was nodding off when you knocked. I'll just brush my teeth.

It was fifteen minutes before she knocked on Anton's slightly ajar door. Heavy breathing came from the far side of the double bed. Carin, removed her dressing gown, latched shut the door and hooked her gown next to Anton's. Walked around to his side of the bed.

Professionally she needed to contain any emotional thoughts, but asleep Anton did look younger than his twenty-eight years.

Owls no longer screeched and soon she was asleep on the opposite side. It was past midnight when Carin was awakened by Anton's arm circled beneath her waist.

'Petra, Petra are you awake? I need to ....' Carin was fully aware of this need and called out,

'Anton, Anton. It's Carin. I can't. I'm not Petra.' At this, Anton removed his arm and withdrew and whipped back the Duvet

'Carin, I'm sorry. I didn't mean to do that?' Carin switched her bedside light on before she realized her nightie was up by her ears. A not uncommon occurrence. She used both hands to pull it down and anchor it beneath her bottom.

'No, Anton. I'm wearing my workaday M&S briefs, fortunately, otherwise, otherwise, well there might have been a little Anton or perhaps Antonia. And who is Petra then?'

'Petra. Did I say Petra. God, that was ages ago. A waitress called Petronella. I can't believe she was in my dreams. Are you alright?' He switched on his bed side light

'I've not been consummated. If I could put it that way.' Carin pulled and released the waistband of her M&S black briefs, like someone might pick at a bullet proof vest that had proved effective.

'But I guess Petra might be disappointed.'

'You're not upset. I mean ...

'Upset for Petra, maybe. It was my idea to share your bed Anton. Don't worry. Perhaps you'd best go to the bathroom, before we go back to sleep. Don't worry Anton. I understand.

I'm with Simon. There's no way I want to put that at risk, anyway. Would I have worn passion killer briefs?' Anton, perhaps didn't share that description of Carin's briefs.

'You're perhaps stressed about seeing your mother in hospital?' Carin reached out to hold his arm, but let go, before he switched out the light and got out of bed to visit the bath room.

# Chapter 26

# Carin Meets Izabella

The following day after Anton paid George for their stay Carin drove into Brodham. The plan was to return to London after the visit to see his mother.

'There's customer parking around the back.' Anton, broke away from the screen, in the back of the Range Rover. A deal was about to go through with a fund investment in an African gold mine. A company which went public a fortnight previously. Sources in the City informed him that a new seam was discovered before the launch. Opportunity for a tidy profit once the news broke. Always, possible boundaries, where insider trading morphs into research, rather than illicit trading. The Range Rover, effectively a mobile office, facilitated instant decision making, although hundreds of miles from the City.

'You could find Izabella interesting.' Anton was not to know that an important mission for Carin was to meet up with Izabella.

'Why is that?' Carin pressed the hand brake button, whilst the unclipped seat belt withdrew.

'She's into cosmetics and fashion.'

'I'd be more interested if it was Formula One racing.'

'Yes, well maybe, but it's probably more interesting than talking about marine valves.'

'I won't argue with that!' She turned and smiled at Anton before she answered a text from Simon with a sad emoji.

Morbid curiosity could not be ruled out as part of the interest in Carin's future meet up with Izabella. Previous investigations revealed that this woman contributed taxes to the British economy not only from the business itself, but also through employment from a local work force. No information available to suggest that Izabella still traded in women slaves. Drugs smuggled through by partner Taras, compromised by security forces, but now of use to security services for a camouflage net to cover defence issues. Ongoing need to deploy the farm storage and transport facilities, that would be out of sight from prying eyes. A deal was most likely at that moment being brokered by Anton, now in his father's office. A young woman spoke earlier with Anton on the way in and she asked if Carin would wait. It wasn't Taras whom she particularly wanted to meet. Carin was directed to an alcove of arm chairs and table which separated two office doors. It was an open plan office, although there were mid - body height cubicles. Female employees, some with headphones, worked at screens. The nearest door opened and an attractive woman, in knee length skirt and suit top, strode out. Carin judged her to be about thirty.

'Carin.' An expensive looking gold bangle, with diamond inserts sparkled under the strip lighting when she held out her hand.

'The men are together to talk about mundane matters of business.' Her hand, moved from hand shake to a gentle clasp of Carin's waist, before she let go. A familiarity which Carin could have done without.

'We can talk about Anton, perhaps?' No, he cannot be my son,' she remarked before she led Carin into her office. She stood with hand out to motion for Carin to sit in a leather office chair next to her own desk.

'He is so much more attractive than his father. But you haven't met Taras?'

'No, I haven't. But Anton is a good person to work for.'

'Ah, I know that it is perhaps what you have to say. Do not worry.' A hand reached out to touch her knee, which would have been totally out of order from a man, but also felt uncomfortable from this woman, whom she'd only just met. A chill shiver needed to be contained. Realization, that she was now in the company of someone, who had no qualms about buying or selling one of her own sex for the slave trade. Was Izabella considering the price that Carin, might fetch in a suitable, dare she say, specialist market?

Carin wasn't met with a hostile response, however. A tray of coffee and biscuits, was in place on the desk. Several cabinets dotted about the office displayed cosmetics, but also knitwear. The door re-opened, following on from Izabella's press of a desk button.

'Heather, when you have poured Mr Carter's Personal Assistant and myself a coffee fetch the cashmere jumper and scarf range for us to see. You can model them.'

'Yes, Izabella, of course.' She smiled at Carin, walked across and set out cups and saucers

'How would you like the coffee?' Carin would rather have dispensed with this formality. Half and half, please Heather.' Whilst she poured two coffees Izabella turned to Carin,

'There're three colours, emerald, cerise and pink. Have you a favourite colour and what size?'

'Emerald suits my black hair,' said Carin. She wanted to appear both friendly and interested,

'I quite like that colour. Medium. But...'

'Bring all three and model the emerald jumper and scarf Heather will you?' Izabella, looked up at Heather as she placed Izabella's coffee in front of her.

'Yes, Izabella.' Heather, turned and went back through the door, closing it behind her.

'It's good to have, a young modern woman, like you in the building to show our products to. You would perhaps like my catalogue to take with you? There is no obligation to buy, you understand it is just out of interest. Izabella picked one from

133

the stack on her desk. And gave it to Carin, when the phone rang.

'No, we cannot help you with exchanges, but please visit the site.' There was a pause.

'Yes, that is it. Your message will be picked up to day. Yes, yes there's also an online chat line, you can go to. Thank you for your call and custom today.'

'These callers they expect the moon on a stick. Never it is a valuable order. But then maybe,' she shrugged her shoulders

'It could lead to bigger things.' Carin reached to pick up the coffee cup when, the door opened and the young woman called Heather entered modelling the emerald jumper and scarf, which she swept back over her shoulder before placing the cerise and pink jumper on the table.

'What size is the jumper you are wearing?'

'Medium,' Heather replied.

'You like that? She said to Carin.

'It's rather nice, yes and in my size.

'You may have it.'

'No,' I mean it must be very expensive.'

'That's okay. You have a boyfriend, partner? Perhaps he'll not like me to give you a present.' It was the insistence in her voice, that made Carin decide to say,

'No, it's not up to him. Thank you very much Izabella.'

'You can have the scarf to match the jumper.' Izabella, extended hand and finger toward Heather.

'Take the jumper off and leave it with the scarf on the desk.' Heather, did as Izabella said, which revealed that she wore just a black bra beneath.

'It would have looked good on Heather with no bra, do you not think?' Heather, a fair haired girl blushed a little more when she said this.' Carin didn't in any way like the way

Izabella spoke to the girl,' but smiled so not to seem at odds. Heather, looked perplexed,and embarrassed, but this didn't bother Izabella.

'Eva, has no problem with modelling, but she is unfortunately on sick leave. It is alright, you can put on this one, before you leave.' She picked up the pink jumper and handed it to Heather.

'They'll wonder what is happening in here, if you return with just a bra. We can't have that can we.' It was what followed that Carin later recalled.

'How is Eva? I want to send some flowers and a get - well card.'

'Martine is to visit. Perhaps you'd better ask her.' There was a rivalry for attention, although Heather would not have wanted to receive the attention given to Eva, if she knew what this entailed. There was no knock on the door from Anton, who walked in after Heather left.

'Anton, it is lovely to see you,' said Izabella. Her face shone like that of a besotted fan on first meet with a pop idol, when she came forward from behind the desk. Anton permitted rather than contributed to the half embrace and cheek kiss from his father's young partner.

Taras fumed about betrayal and how he trusted the Chinese less than the Russian state Police, but now Anton could stabilize his father's mafia activities and bring everything under the umbrella of the British state. It was a compromised result. Protection from rival gangs was something which was needed. After, his apartment was raided, he realized that the security forced were most likely on to his father's activities. The approach after his deal with the Ministry of Transport activities, was in some ways a relief. It was unlikely, he felt to be the Chinese, as his father would have him believe.

'Izabella, I want my PA back.' The emerald green jumper was spread across Carin's lap.

'Izabella's not made you pay for that has she?'

'No, it's a gift for Carin, Anton. I would give one to you,

but we have only women's fashion and cosmetics.'

Carin, not wanting to be the cause of a family rift, quickly responded with

'If you are ever in London, I could show you around, perhaps, Izabella.'

'That would be very nice. When you are not working for Anton. We could go together to enjoy the sights. That I would enjoy in the company of a woman, who has taste. Not that I do not enjoy the company of Anton.' A breath exasperation, from Anton, led to Carin getting to her feet.

'Your chauffeur awaits.'

Chapter 27

# Vicky and Sale of Cleopatra

It's so sad. It's like I'm losing a best friend,' said Vicky

'But you knew Cleo was stabled, that she was up for sale and Annette's, too busy

with work and wanted a buyer. That's why she got you photographed with the horse,

Vicky You'll be in Horse and Hound, again.'

'But I've no interest in a career modelling with a horse. A photo of the rider is just like the part of an extra, anyway. I never thought it would happen so soon. There was I thinking I could have some regular riding and now in a week's time Cleopatra will be out of my life.

'Sounds like you're too attached to that horse, for your own good. And that Anton asked you out again, you said.'

'Did I? what's that got to do with anything?'

'Anyway, Danny will be here soon and here I am – not made the coffee.'

Dot, walked over to place the kettle on the Argo hob and reached into the cupboard for the coffee jar,' whilst Vicky continued to lament the forthcoming departure of Cleo.

'Annette's sold Cleopatra to a Middle Eastern buyer. She's looking for a driver to take him to a FedEx depot. She said I can go in the horse lorry.'

'Probably thinks you'll be a calming influence,' said Dot, as she spooned coffee, then sugar into the green enamel jug and went to fetch the now whistling kettle.

A whine of the postal van's engine in reverse gear could be heard, as Danny manoeuvred into his allocated parking space.

'Not a moment too soon,' she said as she gave the jug a stir and closed the lid.

John, who wasn't listening to the talk between Dot and Vicky but became activated by the van's approach. Got to his feet, pocketed his phone, and walked across to the door.

'I'll be back before seven,' he said. 'The market finishes early.'

'You always say that John Ledley, but no doubt the Three Swans will get a visit before you leave town.'

'What's that phrase they use – networking? I have to network, Dot. Get to know what's happening in the farming world.'

'For my money the only meaningful work in that direction is when fishermen repair their nets.'

Vicky was texting and shortly John could be heard in conversation with Danny outside. Dot placed a tray with a coffee mug and biscuit barrel on the table.

'You say that Annette Hastings is looking for a driver. That'll be for when?'

'A week on Friday.' Three knocks on the door announced Danny's arrival. Dot smiled and called out

'Hi Danny,' as he entered. Careful to wipe his shoes on the indoor mat.

'Busy today?'

'Always Mrs Led these days. West Frampton loves its online shopping.' Vicky remained on her phone, but was now on her feet in preparation for a visit to Cleopatra.

'Are you leaving us Vicky?'

'You know I go to the stable today, mother.'

'I've been thinking.' Danny brought the coffee jug to the table and was about to sit down.

'Been thinking what?' Asked her daughter.

'Danny you must know people at the Post Office who could drive a horse box?'

'When's this for Mrs Led?'

'Friday next,' said Vicky, who realized that this could be a good line of enquiry.

'I hold an HGV licence, if that's any good. And next week I've four days leave due.'

'Danny will want to take his leave, mother,' said Vicky.

'What does it entail?' Danny asked. Dot sat down opposite Danny, but it was Vicky who replied.

'Annette Hastings has sold Cleopatra and she's due delivery to a Fed-ex depot next Friday. That's what it entails. Annette wants me to travel in the cab, but needs a driver. That's what mother's wittering on about.' Danny answered Dot.

'Quite happy to help out, Mrs Led.' Vicky answered.

'You don't have to Danny. You drive all week, anyway.'

'No that's okay, if you don't mind having me for company?'

'Of course, you don't. Don't be silly. Do you Vicky? That would be splendid if you could Danny.'

'No problem. I expect it will be an early start?' Danny, looked toward Vicky for an answer. This was not what she envisioned.

'I'll need to clear it with Annette. Thanks for the offer Danny.

'I'm sure it'll be okay. It's very good of Danny to offer. At such short notice,' said Dot.

Danny an ideal person to accompany her daughter.

# Chapter 28

Carin's curiosity was satisfied, to some extent, you could say, because she had now met Izabella, though not Taras, who remained in his office. Anton leant forward from the back,

mobile in hand, once they were back in the car.

'That's the postcode for our next call,'

'Brodham Hospital – Unit 2' Carin read this out, before she tapped in the code from the address.

'That's it. You're still okay about this visit?'

'Of course, I said I would be, didn't I? A reply endorsed with a smile gave confirmation.

'Are you taking anything for your mother? It's your PA speaking Anton. Perhaps some toiletries. I can select something if you like? Carin pointed to a pharmacy next to a supermarket.

'Okay, put it on this. It's a swipe card. Under thirty pounds, mind He passed Carin the card after she parked.

'I'll get a greetings card?'

Yes, but she'll know it's not me, being that thoughtful.'

'Doesn't matter, Does it? She said. 'And by the way you said - that you'd drive?'

'Okay. Leave the keys in when you've parked.'

Thirty minutes later the car drew into the hospital car park, which was at the side of a large front pillared building. Details, about the establishment were on a board outside. There was no mention of the hospital being a psychiatric unit. Recent NHS policymakers decided that the stigma attached to mental illness needed a more enlightened approach. That patients should be protected from public harassment previously experienced when they were known to attend a psychiatric unit, on their way back into the community.

The word Hospital was followed by "care and rehabilitation unit." A euphemism perhaps for more explicit medical terminology, but progress had been made to update attitudes both in the medical profession and outside toward mental ill - health. Double doors led into a large foyer with seats on both sides of a reception desk. Family groups were sat waiting with individuals. It was visiting time. Anton was given an appointment to see the Charge Nurse and was prepared to wait. Shortly afterwards the receptionist said, after phoning through to the ward,

'Nurse Hatar will be out to see you,' and replaced the phone to continue a scan of a desk screen.

'We'll sit in the waiting area then,' he said, to Carin

'No need, I think.' She'd just caught sight of a dark blue smocked figure slip through doors which led from the ward. A smile in their direction confirmed that he knew who they were and beckoned them over. Away from the waiting area. Nurse Hatar was of Malaysian descent. They'd apparently met. That's Anton and the nurse.

'Anton, your mother will be pleased to see you.' And reached out to shake his hand.

'How is she Nurse?'

'Progressing, she's in a meeting group. Perhaps you'd like to wait in the view area with –

'Carin's my Personal assistant,' said Anton. 'We're on a business trip.'

'Most pleased to meet you Carin.' Nurse Hatar gave a slight bow. Carin replied with

'And you. It's alright for me to join Anton?'

'Most certainly. It's good that we have visitors on the Mantovani suite. Would you please follow me, then?'

'Mantovani? Didn't he have an orchestra – way back?' Asked Carin.' They walked toward the ward entrance

'Yes, you're quite right,' Nurse Hatar, turned in reply. Anton, quiet, with memory of a previous visit.

'Yes, the name and music help create a soothing atmosphere. That was the thinking. It can be challenging on a Mantovani suite, even so,' he said, accompanied with a smile, before opening a double door by remote control. The second door required access through a door pad combination.

On entry into the first part of the ward, gentle music wafted down from speakers, before they arrived at a pale green door. It was numbered five with the two letters VP beneath. Curiosity answered when the charge nurse said,

'We can go into the "View platform," whilst we wait for the meeting to end.'

A buzzer sounded on entry and a desk spotlight made visible an assistant, sat at a station, to the left of the view glass. She reached up to remove a right ear phone. An identical unoccupied position on the right

'Nurse Tipah, we will join you for a while.' A hand raised and the ear piece was replaced. Anton and Carin were directed toward the middle of a line of chairs. Nurse Hatar sat next to Anton.

'You can see Alsa, your mother - yes?'

'Yes,' said Anton. A group of twelve sat in front of a flip chart addressed. Half wore dressing gowns. Alsa, was dressed, but alert. Others were fairly well sedated to judge by the expressionless vacant look in eyes. A young woman was out front talking to the group and the tutor, a slightly older woman, could be seen to thank her. Then take hold of her arm, which caused her to pull away. Nurse Hatar said,

'What's going on Tipah? Why's she having a go at the tutor.'

'She said that she didn't want another woman to touch her.'

'It's Eva, isn't it?'

'Yes, she's voluntarily in the group for a day. It was decided that the discussion group might be therapeutic for her. Oh, look she's leaving. I'll go and see if she's alright before she goes home.'

Alsa and some of the others stood up, but the tutor raised and lowered her hands for them to sit down. Nurse Tipah opened a nearby door and faced Eva with a look of concern. Both about the same age. Eva comforted by her presence left the room.

'They're returning to the community room. We'll go to see Alsa now. She's much better now said Nurse Hatar.

'Yes,' said Anton. Outside in the corridor it was Carin who asked,

'Why are half the patients in dressing gowns?'

'They've to earn the right to wear day clothes. Alsa, is much better now. That is why she is in her day clothes.'

'That, must be good, then,' said Anton. Further along the corridor they entered a red carpeted room with a mixture of red sofas and upholstered chairs. It might have been the main room of a stately house. The group had returned to the ward, area, but Alsa, was sat with another woman with dark hair, no more than thirty.

There were several nurses and hospital staff in attendance. Two patients played table tennis at the far end, and a few sat in alcoves did appear to be reading. Others stared vacantly. It was not quite, as Carin imagined a secure ward in a hospital to be.

'Anton, is here to see you with Carin,' said Nurse Hatar.

'Anton!' She got unsteadily to her feet and kissed his cheek, before sitting back down. Nurse

Hatar held the arm of the settee and leant forward.

'How are you Julie?' You look, so much more relaxed.

'I'm down from cloud seven, if that's what you mean.'

'Mother, you are also looking more relaxed as well.' Anton sat down in a chair opposite to his mother

Carin sat nearer to Julie.

'You, have been away a long time, Anton. When can I return to the flat with Alexia? Alexia being Alsa's older sister.

'First things first. You're getting better. Nurse Hatar is really pleased with your progress.'

'I'll leave you to talk for a while,' said the Nurse, and whispered in Anton's ear,

'No more, than half an hour, you understand. They're due to have a meal and medication.'

'Okay, that's fine,' said Anton. Alsa, raised a hand toward Carin.

'That young woman, is she your wife Anton?' Carin gave a polite smile.

'No, she helps at work.'

'You do need a wife Anton. You won't always be able to pick and choose.' For someone not that mentally stable these were wise words.

'Julie helps me in the painting class. You should see her still life paintings. She's professionally trained, you know.' Julie, sat cross-legged. A trim figure, mid- thirties, in tee shirt, washed jeans and pink trainers. Carin didn't want to directly ask about Julie's situation, but after she said,

'You're both in outdoor clothes?' Julie, explained, anyhow.

'Part of the problem for us is that with no visible injury people don't really believe, anything's wrong until something kicks off. I get like euphoric and sort have to come down to earth.'

'Like on a high?' asked Carin.

'Yes, but there're no drugs. Well perhaps ones that my mind makes itself. Oh, I'm on medication now. You heard the charge nurse say that there's medication due. They brought me in by ambulance. That's what they told me, anyhow. I believed it to be a space ship at the time. That I was in a space suit getting aboard when they picked me up. I knew looking back that I was near to a trip. I mean gone euphoric. Pebbles, that's my cat, snarled and spat all of a sudden.'

'Who's looking after Pebbles now?' Asked Carin.

'A young couple on the next floor up. Pebbles is always in and out. He just takes up residence. When I get back, he climbs out of their window and looks in. If he thinks I look safe to be with he taps on the window.' Anton asked about his mother and how, when she could live in the relative luxury of a Priory that she'd moved to Brodham.

'I wasn't going to stand back and let that Izabella have everything. Aunt Alexia came with me. She visits and brings me Russian dessert? She says it's like being sent to Siberia, but the heating's good.' A middle - aged man walked across and Julie called out,

'Welcome back Timothy.' He smiled and carried on walking.

'Timothy periodically gorges on cushion foam and has to be pumped out.'

'That's a medical condition called Pica isn't it?' said Carin who knew of the condition. Awareness that patients could become institutionalized quite quickly and Timothy was probably one such patient.

'Didn't know that,' said Julie. Anton, continued talking to his mother.

'Have they said when you might be out of this secure unit mother?' Alsa, arrived back from listening to what Julie was saying to Carin, but not sufficiently to understand fully what was asked. Attention drifted. Anton changed the question.

'Has anyone said how long you'll be here and will Alexia be visiting soon.

'Alexia, she visits when she can. Alexia is going to talk with Dr Evans, next time, Anton.

'It's up to Dr Evans, but Alexia is going to talk with him next week. Tell your father, Anton, that he is only separated not divorced. When the divorce comes through, he will be free to run around after Izabella, all the time. I will not miss him, but I worry for you Anton, that you have such a father. I think you have more of my family blood and you have done well in honest business ventures.' Alsa was divorced, but had retreated to an earlier situation, in her mind. Carin's ears pricked up, but she said nothing. She took the get well card from her hand bag, removed its envelope and handed it together with a pen to Anton.

'Your Carin, is very thoughtful. I don't think that is you Anton?'

'You're a very considerate young woman. I would like a daughter like you very much.'

Anton signed the card and Carin asked,

'Do you have a locker? There's a few things here you might find useful.' Nurse Hatar returned at this point.

'You're very fortunate, you know to have visitors Alsa that bring gifts and a card. It's nearly time to leave.' He smiled at Anton.

'I'll visit next time I'm here. Perhaps at your apartment, yes? Said Anton.

'You are lucky Alsa,' said Julie. Anton, kissed his mother on the cheek and got up. Carin handed the carrier with toiletries to the Nurse for safe-keeping.

'It's been so nice to meet you Alsa.'

'And you Carin. I hope you stay with Anton.'

'Carin isn't with me mother, she's my Personal Assistant.'

'And chauffeur,' said Carin.

'One more step perhaps and you could have a third role, then' said Alsa.

'But Carin has a boyfriend, mother.

'A girl will say these things to a man. She likes to see him compete, you know.'

'No, I don't know what you're talking about? I'm glad to see that you're making good progress in getting better, though.

# Chapter 29

# Annette with Izabella

Izabella's request to visit was not unexpected. Business cards were exchanged at the first Maria Agrande Dance class. Half-way through the dance class and Izabella texted.

'NXT Thurs is ok?' Izabella explained to Annette, when together at dance classes, that there were certain products she needed to prepare photos for.

'Would she be interested in a percentage payment from sales if she photographed them first.' A photo studio was already set up in Annette's second bedroom, which over looked paddock and stables. Her main bedroom was roadside, which enabled Annette to see anyone who approached.

It was the purr from a yellow soft top Merc that brought her to the bedroom window. In time to see the driver's car door swing open. By the time Izabella entered through the post office door Annette was behind the counter.

'Izabella you've made the visit at last. We planned this weeks ago. it's quiet I can shut up shop for a while.'

'Can you Nettie. That's good. I've some business for you.' Izabella reached into a hessian bag and produced ten A4 sized envelopes.

'They're second class, but the carrier is very expensive for these envelopes.'

'Just place one on the scale and I'll give you a price. How many are there?'

'There's ten. It's a lovely cottage you have here. Taras, is so difficult to move, but I could enjoy living in somewhere like this. If you ever want to sell?'

'Not just now, Izabella.'

'The envelopes are all the same.'

'Place one on the scales.' Annetta lifted the window and took the remainder. Checked that they went through the envelope measuring slot

'That will be seven pounds fifty. My cottage is not for sell, but you can have first offer if I ever do want to sell.'

'That I would like.'

Annetta attached labels to envelopes and dropped them into the collection. Izabella paid with a ten - pound note

'Izabella it's nice of you to visit. I've Vicky from a nearby farm here to look after Cleo, but I pay her to do this. it's different, you understand?

'Yes, I understand Nettie. Is it just on Tuesday?'

'No, Cleo needs three days of exercise. I've a gardener who mucks out and Vicky is here on Thursday and Friday after-noons, as well. Must remember, postman arrives shortly, but I'll see him from upstairs.' Seconds later a dull thud came from an opened door bolt. Annette turned the key already in the lock.

'Welcome to my cottage Izabella.' After securing the door, Annette led Izabella along a carpeted corridor with pictures of rosetted horses. Annette in riding dress in some.

'You are also a successful horse rider.'

'I was much younger.'

'But you keep the skill, no. Is there a good - sized other room and kitchen?' I can see that the post office was once the living room yes?

'That's right. Except for a small extension to the front.' Annette moved ahead and opened a door on the right to show Izabella her dining room.

'It's a good size.'

'You'll have to visit when the shop is closed, Izabella. I like to view from upstairs when I leave the counter

'Your cottage appeals more and more, Nettie. Where do we go now?'

'Annette opened a door, which led to a stairway, which intrigued Izabella.

'Perhaps its best I lead the way,' Annetta took hold of the bannister rail.

'Maybe a family with three or four children lived here, no?' Izabella said as she followed.

'They might have Izabella, but that's not for me – children – that is.'

'Perhaps we're like soul persons, Nettie. Taras, I've told him no more. He has the son Anton from a first marriage. That's enough, and I would be with a younger man if I wanted children. Annetta reached the short strip of landing, turned and said,

'You're so right Izabella. I've nephews and nieces. They're more than enough.' Izabella kissed her on the cheek. To Annetta a snatched cheek kiss, didn't seem that inappropriate. After all. It could have been in Russian culture for women to spontaneously kiss. In the way that a spontaneous kiss, from a relatively new British friend could feel inappropriate.

'Your curate friend might want you to provide him with a family.' Annetta laughed.

'It's nowhere near that. He would need him to be a vicar before I even considered him as a partner. For me Izabella a man would need to be useful to have around, but once married they can become irritatingly needy and controlling.

'I cannot argue with you Nettie. Oh, this second bedroom has so much space.' Izabella walked into a bedroom, with a fitted blue carpet. A variety of black hooded spotlights on the far right with stands that held blue, white and red photo boards for backdrops. She walked across to one of the two windows. Cord tasselled restraints held back faded gold curtains. There down in the paddock she saw Vicky, mount Cleopatra. The gate into the next field was held back with baling string. The mare stamped, anxious to be away. Vicky leant forward above the saddle, whilst the horse wheeled a bit, but calmed down when she could be seen speaking to it. Izabella smiled to herself. Yes, she understood how an Arab prince could be equally entranced. Unlikely, to be incinerated, in a Tandoori oven, while she remained that attractive.

'A lovely view of the countryside, as well.' No mention that she had seen Vicky.

'And this is where you photograph for online display. It looks ideal and very professional.

'Thank you, for saying so.' Annetta, crossed over and opened the door to her bedroom to look down to the pavement below. Danny strode up the path from behind Izabella's Merc. He opened a mail bag prior to clearing the walled post box.

'I'll have to leave you for a little while. The postman is here.'

'That's perfectly alright. It's a very beautiful view from the window.' Once Annetta was downstairs Izabella contacted the group designated by Oleg and Yakov.

'Yes, I have three days -Tuesday, Thursday and Friday afternoon. There was a pause.

'No, that cannot be guaranteed. A sale needs to takes place. Otherwise opportunity will pass. Another pause.

'No, I will not return here. There will be no connection. I have built trust with the woman, anyway. I wait first reply. First reply, now you understand.' This was understood as a first payment of fifty thousand. It was on her return from Post responsibilities that Annetta received a call. She stopped on the stairs.

'Yes, that's right. There's concrete standing and facilities. Her agents were asking about reservations for motor home visitors to stay this Friday.

'You have good references? She asked the agents. A pause and

'Yes. The space is available.

'No, why should I worry that they're Chinese. They're

probably more civilized than some of our native population.

'Okay, next Friday. Bye.' Sorry,' she called up to Izabella. 'But, it's good news. I've a week's booking for a motor home next week. But they might only stay a few days. Also Cleopatra has a buyer from an advert in Horse and Hound.'

'Perhaps, I bring you good luck in business Nettie. Might I ask favour from you. I have to go to see a sick uncle in Vladivostok after next week. My online business can be left with Taras, but you know a man knows nothing about cosmetics. There're questions from customers that need to be answered by a woman with sophistication. Yes, my staff they can answer questions about the catalogue and prices. It would just need for you to visit, perhaps once or twice, Nettie. Unexpectedly would be good. I would pay for this work, of course. Do you think you could manage this? You said, at dance class, that you have a woman from the village who looks after the post office on three mornings. I do not want to impose, you understand. I would show you the system we use. It's not complicated.' Shared acquaintanceship with their membership of the Tango dance group undoubtedly compromised Annetta's ability to refuse Izabella's request.

'Yes, I expect that'll be alright, but you will need to show me what you want me to do.'

'Of course. Would next Tuesday be suitable to visit, in the morning?'

'Where are your premises, exactly?'

'You know where Taras has his Marine store in Brodham. My and his offices and packing area are on the top floor. I can show you how messages are received. There're standard responses. I will deal with difficult ones when I return, of course. It would be just for two days each week for a fortnight. Taras would not let me stay away any longer.'

'Yes, I have Motor Home visitors to be settled on Friday. Tuesday would be a good day. That's in the morning. I have to be back by twelve - thirty.' Annette led the way down to the corridor to the main office.

'It will work well because I've a few products which I need to be photographed.'

'You can show them to me and I'll take them and send you a jpeg for approval.'

'That is good. I will so look forward to your visit Nettie,' said Izabella as she stepped out of the post office on to the pavement.

'It has been so nice for me to see your post office and cottage. Next Tuesday. I will see you again then.'

# Chapter 30

# Anton and Carin Leave Hospital

As previously decided Anton drove out of the hospital. Carin turned to Anton.

'Your mother has your aunt to stay with,' said Carin. 'They share an apartment. That's when she's not at the hospital?'

'Yes, that's a saving factor. My father likes to believe he's moved on, but without her sister, my mother would be on her own.'

'She's got you Anton.'

'Yes, but hundreds of miles away, except when I visit on business.'

'Perhaps, we could arrange some more visits.'

'It was good of you to come along with me, Carin.'

'It's in the PA area of involvement. We're going back, now aren't we?'

'Yes. That's why I said I'd drive.' Anton turned and smiled at Carin.'

'Don't you trust my driving at night,' she replied.

'It's not that. But you've had the same long day as me. I'm not a slave driver.'

'Anton, could we stop at the pharmacy by the supermarket?'

'Yes sure.'

'Is there anything you need?'

'No. I'll wait in the car. I've a few messages to make.'

Ten minutes later, Anton, parked the Range Rover in the supermarket car park. The pharmacy was a single story building a hundred yards from the main car park.

'I won't be long. Sure there's nothing you want? Carin

asked after she released her seat belt and opened the door.

'No. We can have a break at a motorway service station.'

'Okay. Don't drive off and forget me, will you?

'You're not going to be that long----?'

'No.'

'Okay.' A hoped - for deeper level of attachment in Anton's reply wasn't forthcoming. Carin walked past a wooded section with the exit road behind, and then into the entrance which led toward the pharmacy. Unfamiliar with the shop lay out several minutes passed whilst she tracked down the items required.

When she left overhead lights cast a subdued yellow tinge over everything. There were no cars around the Range Rover. Nor was an interior light visible. Carin approached from the passenger door side. It was only then that she saw Anton slumped across the steering wheel with left hand grasped on his right. Instinctively she walked around and tapped on the window. An overhead light picked out blood that had seeped through his fingers. He was conscious. This could have only have happened minutes before she returned. Anton was able to lower the window.

'Anton what's happened?'

'They've shot me. I don't think it was meant for my arm, but I moved it when the windows were lowered. I thought somehow, I'd triggered the windows open, but they must have access to the mechanism. There was no noise. The gun must have been silenced. I heard a motor bike start. Carin on your side, there's a First aid kit in the glove box.' Carin returned, to the passenger side. Opened the glove box and remover a green First Aid box. Returned and re-opened Anton's door.

'I've scissors in my handbag. I'll need to cut away your jacket and apply a tourniquet above the wound.'

'Aren't you going to ask who shot me?'

'More's to the point we need to get you to an emergency

hospital with that bullet in your arm.'

'It's not.' Anton pointed with his left arm to a tear in the side of the passenger seat.'

'It's in there somewhere.' Carin momentarily turned and blinked away tears.

'Look once I've seen to this do you think you can move across to the passenger side.'

'Who do you think did shoot you then?'

'Let's say my father has enemies.'

'Right.' Carin stuffed the cut away shirt and jacket arm under the seat and made Anton hold a dressing over the wound whilst she wrapped a bandage down from his shoulder to cover the dressing and wound. Once completed she returned to the passenger side and helped move Anton across.

'Look we could call an ambulance, but the sooner we get you to see a doctor the better. I'll drive straight to the hospital. It's the one we passed on the way to see your mother, isn't it?'

'Yes, but father has a private consultant. The police are bound to get involved once it's explained what's happened.'

'Not necessarily. It will be kept secret.'

'I don't understand.' Carin started the engine and started to drive toward the exit.

'Anton, I need to explain. I work for the security services.'

'What security services? You're a spy?'

'Not quite that straightforward. But there is inter- state action and I was placed,'

'Like a sleeper?'

'Yes, you could say that. Certainly, this has awakened me. When we arrive at the hospital emergency services I'll be in contact with my department to make sure that the hospital is under surveillance and that no questions are asked about your injury. All of this can be arranged. I can't tell you more at the moment. You'd best stay the night at the hospital.'

'With police protection?'

'They're more discrete. You'll not know anyone's there. I've some catching up to do and will return to the Trellis and Vine afterwards. Anton, I really think you need specialist treatment – at a hospital. I'll explain more later.'

# Chapter 31

# Carin Books in at the Trellis and Vine

It was half an hour's drive from the hospital to the Trellis and Vine. There was disappointment in George's voice when Carin booked in by herself to stay the night.

'Just yourself, not Mr Carter.'

'That's right George. He's been taken away on urgent business.' No further explanation was given to Anton before Carin left in the Range Rover. Her orders were to return to the pub and re-connect once in the car park. Further details of the shooting were given and before she left there was a pause and then,

'We'll need to check out that vehicle you're driving. There's likely to be a tracking device. On arrival, undipped headlights picked out the hedge either side which led into the pub car park. Carin drove past cars, scattered in the middle, to the far end, which faced a field. A space was left by a motorhome with a motorcycle strapped to its back. The Range Rover's front wheels were against the kerb when she stopped. Drawl from the engine died and with all lights switched off, doors secured, Carin re-connected as instructed.

'Okay, where are you parked?'

'In the Trellis and Vine car park at the far end. Vehicle faced towards a field. There's a motor home, nearby. Guess the owners are inside the pub.'

'When you leave, place the key under the front driver's wheel. We'll get someone out to check it out. Stay in the bar for a while. Veronica wants to talk with you. She'll return the key.'

'I didn't realize that there was this level of monitoring. Is it because Anton Carter's been shot?'

'No, it's more about Izabella. Veronica will put you in the picture.'

'Is it gang warfare?'

'That's ongoing. Can't say more, but Anton's father has dealings with the Chinese and they might have decided to take him out.'

'But they didn't succeed,' said Carin. The bullet looked intended for Anton's upper body, not arm.'

'These are interstate issues. There will be collateral incidents.' A statement that chilled Carin, but she knew it to be true.

'Book for the night.'

'I've done that.'

'Alright. Reports are that your boss, in the civilian world, will be released tomorrow. We'll decide whether you can return to London. These and other issues Veronica will discuss with you.'

'And what are they?'

'It's better that Veronica talks to you. Woman to woman.'

'That's sexist.'

'Not intended, but she'll be better qualified to handle what's going to be asked of you.'

'Because, she's a woman?'

'Yes, that does come into it. Viv le difference, is all I can say,' and the line closed.

A car drove into the entrance just as Carin entered through the ivied entrance of the pub A lone woman who entered a pub might have seemed out of place. As, Carin entered the bar area Carol, though smiled back in recognition. Carin walked across, overnight bag in hand.

'Hi Carol. I'm expecting to meet a friend, a bit later. I'm booked in for the night.' She said.

'Hi – Nice to see you again. I'll just go and let George

know.' She left the bar and came back a minute or two later with a room key.

'It's the same room you were in before, Carin, number four. She ducked down behind the bar and re-appeared with the visitor's book. If you just sign in, If that's okay. Here's the key.' She placed it on the opened book. I'm on my own until Vicky arrives.'

'I've not met Vicky, have I?'

'No, she's back from Uni. Three afternoons a week she's exercises Cleo.'

'Cleo?'

'A horse, that belongs to the Sub-postmistress at West Frampton.' It was then just chat and meant nothing to Carin.

'Thanks Carol,' she signed her name, Carin Hanson, with the biro tied to the spine of the book – and picked up the room key. Not offended that little fuss was made about her arrival. It was the way it needed to be. Memories of that previous visit flooded back as she mounted the stairs to number four bedroom. Anton, unaware of her true identity, then. Now what would be the consequences? Sad eyes, betrayed that need for steeliness, as Carin stood by the wardrobe mirror.

Veronica would make up some story about meeting up with an old school friend, to Carol. The fact, that Carin was to meet another woman and not a man was probably more appropriate. Veronica and Mike, shared dual power roles, in the service. Not their real names. Career advancement, Carin previously felt, could have come from this role to track Anton. Mike didn't tell her off for giving away true identity, but would they allow her to stay in the position of PA? She changed out of her business suit, covered by an overcoat, on arrival into jeans, jumper and a light navy corduroy jacket. Discrete, and ignorable, she decided would be best, when in the Lounge bar. Veronica was being served by Carol and the young woman that she assumed to be Vicky served two

Asians. A man and a woman. Veronica, looked tall next to the Asians and Carin heard her say,

'Yes, a slice of lemon, as well,' on arrival at her side. Neat and vocal best described Veronica for Carin. Men might exchange neat for fit, but they would need to like endless chatter. Carin didn't know a man's perspective about making love to a woman. Even when viewed as potentially heavenly and fit, he might consider that a gag on Veronica's mouth, necessary, even if she was the one that instigated sex. Veronica wore a gold buttoned blazer and jeans. Hair, neatly plaited and folded.

'Carin, just a fleeting visit. I got your message that you were staying at the Trellis. Carol told me that you'd arrived. Will it be the usual for you?

'Yes, Veronica, that'll be fine.'

'Make that a white wine, as well.' Carin, discovered her "usual" drink to be white wine.

'There's a table free over there.' Veronica pointed to a table by the fireplace away from the bar. Carin had never met Veronica socially, before. Normally, she would be joined with Mike at headquarters, but still managed most of the talking, then.

'We can bring your drinks over,' said Carol.

'How much?' asked Veronica.

'That'll be six pound and sixty please.'

Veronica, removed a card from her handbag and waved it across the card machine.

'That's through,' said Carol, only for Veronica loudly to say,

'Come along, we've got so much to talk about.' Carin followed Veronica.

'That's better we're out of hearing.' she said. Pointed to a chair opposite before she sat down.

'You look a little drained Carin.'

'I've just taken Anton Carter to hospital with a gun shot

wound. What do you expect?' Carin not meaning to snap continued with,

'I've also blown cover, which could've been avoided.'

'No, Carin. You did the right thing. The last thing we wanted was to have the local police involved. Anton Carter wouldn't have wanted to go public and we certainly don't. As it is, we need you to pick him up from hospital. That vehicle will have been checked over. We ran a check on that Motor Home parked nearby That couple sat over there are Colonel's in the People's Republic of China. We've made a connection with Izabella through the transfer of funds. They're not here to view the English countryside, that's for sure.' Veronica looked around.

'I do rather like this bar. It was a good choice Carin.' Veronica said this just as Vicky approached with a drinks tray.

'Will you be having anything else? There's a bar menu.' She'd picked up a menu from an adjoining table, and placed it on the table together with the drinks. The polished tray reflected from a wall mounted light.

'Not just at the moment, but thank you,' said Veronica. Vicky returned to the bar.

'Delightful young woman?'

'Yes, very pleasant,' said Carin.

'We're not the only ones to think that. But, more on that later.'

'Here's to the future.' Veronica raised her glass. Carin took a sip and returned the glass to the table.

'Who's future, in particular?' Carin sensed that something more was expected from her.

'You and Anton Carter, Carin.'

'What do you mean. I work for him as his Personal Assistant.'

'And Chauffeur. And you shared his bed I understand.' Veronica looked towards the ceiling.

'In this very place.'

'Shared, but that was it. I've not had sex for Queen and Country – if that's what you're making out, Veronica.'

'Carin.'

'Yes?'

'Bad news on the Simon front. Whilst you're away he's around at a female work colleague's flat.'

'I had my suspicions.'

'Good.'

'How's that Veronica?'

'We have a proposition to make, which would lead to a higher pay grade immediately vows were in place.'

'What vows by whom and to whom?'

'A registry office marriage to Anton. You could have something in the service like – "to be good friends forever." No, binding declaration and in a year or two a divorce would be organized. Look Carin, I don't think Anton would find this a bad deal. You won't be expected to lie like back and think of England. There's no need for emotional attachment from either side.

'Like it's some business deal?'

'Well give it consideration Carin. Not too long because we'd like you to suggest this to Anton when you fetch him from the hospital tomorrow.'

'Yikes, how can you do this Veronica? How can you suggest this just after Simon's done the dirty on me. And you want me to ask him in the hospital?'

'Well get him back here. Lay the ground work. Come on Carin. You must have known that whenever you were gone away any length of time, Simon was playing away.'

'No, I didn't. Well, I partly blame myself for being away. I did have suspicions – but tried not to believe them.'

'You don't come across as heart - broken. Moving away from that – that Vicky now a barmaid, she's been bought for a middle eastern prince. Details are that he dated her whilst he was getting a British degree.'

'They were together at Uni. And now he can blatantly do this?

'That's it they weren't together, in the sense of girlfriend, boyfriend. It's like he's paid for stalkers and kidnappers. There are intermediaries to arrange a kidnap.

'How do you know this?

A certain Oleg and Yakov.'

'The two I never got to meet?'

'Same two. They've somehow got wind of Taras's tie up with the state. You could say that they've cashed in their chips, because they don't trust Izabella.'

'Don't tell me. Izabella is behind the kidnap.'

'Not exactly. She's in the way of facilitator. That's according to those two. Fifty thousand - pound payments flashed through to an account in Vladivostok in her name.'

'Where do the Chinese Colonels' come in to this? Carin's hand raised a finger to indicate how they were on a nearby table.

'Not sure, but they most likely fired at Anton. But, we're not totally certain. The bullet removed from the seat will help.'

'How, on earth did this Arab prince track the girl down?'

There's an internet shopping list of persons. They're listed as trophies. Persons wanted to be bought, across different regions. Young women mainly, but also, men. Some are TV stars. This girl's photo came up and these two, that's Oleg and Yakov, recognized her'

'And they brought Izabella into the deal?

'Yes. The two Chinese were most likely involved with the shooting of Anton.'

'Not, us?'

'No.' Carin's tense look, relaxed.

'The Chinese side of things seem to be involved with

163

threats to Cocaine supplies. They wanted to get at Taras, we think and kill Anton. This is supposition.'

'But the girl could still be taken. And she'll end up on the missing person's list.'

'There is that possibility.'

'Marked down as an ongoing police investigation? I'll get another drink,' said Carin, 'and it won't be white wine.'

'I'll not have another, but go ahead. You're not having anywhere to drive to.'

Carin walked across the long strip of floor to the bar. Both girls were serving customers, but managed to talk, whilst they selected glasses and drinks. Carin listened.

'You'll tell Danny tomorrow that it's cancelled, won't you? Said Vicky, who took money for an order before Carol replied with,

'I don't see why you can't message him?'

'Carol, he 'll be here first before he goes to the post office. Annetta can explain to him that

Cleopatra wasn't ready and anyway the buyer's cancelled the sale.'

'That'll be nine – eighty,' Carin said to the couple whose drinks she'd prepared before she turned across to Vicky

'Alright, if you like. Still, don't see why you can't message him yourself.'

'We just don't text. It's a business arrangement and I'll be able to continue exercising Cleopatra. Mother arranged it anyhow. Danny was to drive that's all.'

'Okay.' Carol realized that Carin was waiting to be served.

'Oh, sorry.' Said Carol, 'didn't see you there – another white wine?'

'There's no hurry. My friend's leaving shortly and I'm ready for bed. Is it possible to have a hot chocolate?

'Of course. I'll get it ready. Would you like it taken up to your room?'

'No, could you bring it over. It can go on the bill I presume?'

'Oh, yes, no problem. Suzi, said to ask what time would you like breakfast?'

'Is eight -thirty, okay? Asked, Carin.

'You'll be first – that's the start time.' She returned to the table.

'No drink?' said Veronica.

'I'm having hot chocolate. Full day tomorrow.' Veronica continued,

'Yes, that vehicles checked out. We'd like you to pick Anton up and return here.

'Tell him, when you find a moment that you've instructions to return to your role, as PA on condition that he agrees to marry you. We've discussed this.'

'Veronica! It's beyond the line of duty.'

'Not, Carin, if you want to stay operational and continue in metaphor speak - stay in the field. I'd have no problem with this in your position. You can lay the ground rules. His father and now Izabella are in our sights, but they serve a purpose.' Vicky arrived with hot chocolate and a plate of assorted biscuits. She placed the tray on the table.

'Thank you, said Carin, with a smile. 'That's just what I 've been looking forward to.' And once out of hearing,

'Look if Izabella's taking cash to facilitate that girl's kidnap she can be held and charged can't she?' Veronica raised a hand.

'Not so fast, she's friends with the Russian President. The best we can do is stop the kidnap Ultimately prevent them taking her out of the UK. You'll have their confidences once you've secured a marriage deal to Anton. We'll remain in contact. Carin, you'll be safer now than if you were discovered as a spy by Izabella. You do see that?

'Yes and no. What if Anton rejects the idea of a bogus marriage?'

'You have to make him want to say yes.'

'And if I succeed in winning him over?'

'Just text me with "Yes." I'll make sure you're on a new pay grade the moment you sign the marriage registry. Can't you see it'll work really well. You can continue your PA role and with no affection for the guy you can keep your personal life separate.'

'Yes, that's possible, but only if he agrees.'

'He'll see it as a good business arrangement Carin. Don't worry.'

Chapter 32

# Anton's Fetched from Hospital

Carin, went to the bar, after Veronica left. Carol, farther away was chatting to Vicky and she waved a thank you. Carin left her number at the hospital, but there'd been no call. Anton, could be asleep or under anaesthetic. Without Veronica's visit she would have phoned earlier. It wasn't 'til After she'd locked her bedroom door that Carin keyed in the code to Anton's phone. After several rings he answered.

'Carin.'

'Hi Anton. How are you?'

'They've cleaned and stitched the wound and I've to take anti-biotics. Thought you might have gone back to your base and left me.'

'You knew I wouldn't do that. I've new instructions or I would have called earlier.

'Still on the case? -That's me, presumably?'

'Look Anton we can't talk over the phone. I'm your Personal Assistant and I've booked an early breakfast to get over to see you. It's perhaps best that we book another night at the Trellis. I mean how do you feel?'

'A bit groggy, but they seem to be keen for me to leave tomorrow.'

'I need to put you in the picture about developments. Your car's been given the okay.'

'I never knew there was anything wrong with it.'

'That's one thing we need to talk about. I'll pick you up hopefully before ten and I'll book in for another night. Separate rooms, as before.'

'Will you want to share my bed?'

'That's not planned, but we can talk back here tomorrow. Are you in pain? I mean it's terrible what's happened. Who could have done this?' Carin maintained an unfamiliarity with who Anton was associated with, although she knew there were explanations needed, not least in matters of future relationships between her and Anton.

'The ever - caring PA, Carin. There's just a numbness down the arm. Like I've been clubbed by something heavy.'

'What about your father. Has he been told about this?

'Yes, but in the circumstances, I said for him not to visit. You'll need to talk with him.'

'Feel very tired. Look forward to seeing you tomorrow Carin. Bye.' A click came down the line. Carin prepared for sleep. Trauma can have different effect on individuals. Anton seemed unalarmed, but this could change. There was another distinct change after Carin was finishing breakfast and Veronica phoned.

'Have you contacted Anton Carter yet?'

'In my capacity of his PA, yes Veronica. I'm to fetch him from hospital and then we're to stay for a night at the Trellis and Vine.'

'Good work, Carin.'

'It's not like that. I mean this is normal procedure that a PA might follow. I'll have to find a suitable moment.'

'That suitable moment is ASAP, Carin and by the way the tracker on that Motor Home, with the Chinese couple has traced it to the field behind West Frampton sub post office.'

'Really. Well it makes sense that they call in at the Trellis and Vine then for an evening meal.

It's not far up the road.

'We know they're here on a tour of British village churches and leave today, Friday. Let me know how it goes with Anton – won't you?'

'Yes, Veronica – bye.'

Carin said – "weird," out loud. What interest would main land Chinese have in Village Churches? As she left the breakfast room adjoined to the bar George called across.

'Everything will, be ready for Mr Carter. It's perfectly alright for him to have number five room again. That'll be later today.'

'Yes, I'm to pick him up, very shortly.' No mention had been made of Anton's stay in Hospital, but she said,

'Mr Carter has a sporting injury. Nothing serious, but needs some rest before we return to London.'

'So sorry to hear that. You'll be back shortly then.

'Yes, if that's alright.'

'Perfectly.'

'Might I ask what sport?'

'Polo.'

There were no further questions, but the impressed look on George's face returned the answer Carin was looking for. Hands trembled whilst buttoning the white blouse that she wore under her suit coat. What was Anton likely to say? "with no affection for the guy," were Veronica's words, not Carin's. Other than curiosity there was no particular reason why Carin googled for a view of West Frampton Sub Post office. The overview showed a cottage. Greenery on the trees meant it was summer and there was a Motor Home parked, in the place where the Chinese Motor Home would now be due to leave today, Friday. It was the stable adjacent to the concreted motor home area that reminded Carin that this was where the girl Vicky went to exercise the horse named Cleopatra. Anton heard a motor bike start up. Yes - there was a bike on the motor home. Visits to the Trellis and Vine a reconnoitre? But was this just wild imagination?

Although, shocked and horrified by what had happened to Anton her mind was set on a visit to the West Frampton Post office in the hope to find that fear for this young woman's safety was unfounded. That she was under no risk when innocently she attended to exercise a horse, stabled next to a certain motor home.

There were two nurses attending to Anton, who was dressed and sat in a chair in the single hospital room. She introduced herself as Carin, Personal assistant.

'He's such a good patient,' said the older one, who was probably more senior and entering notes on a clip board. The young one smiled at Anton whilst taking his pulse. Carin felt a twinge of jealousy. Anton was getting a kind of attention that energized Carin to get him out as quickly as possible. On their return, to the Trellis and Vine he talked about work back in the London office. It was only just before they entered the pub door that he said,

'Carin, there's one hell of a lot of explaining that you need to do.' After she once again signed the visitor's book, but on Anton's behalf due to his writing arm injury, they went to bedroom number five.

'Without my being shot, you'd never have said anything?' Anton was sat opposite to Carin in the bedroom alcove window.

'No, but we're on your side. You do want to extricate your father from this mafia – style life?'

'Yes of course.' He winced as he attempted to get seated more comfortably.

'Oh, Anton.' Carin, momentarily, broke from her executive demeanour, reached across to touch his good arm.

'You are a good person to work for. This is terrible and I want to stay in this role, if you can accept that my appointment was to ensure the Department of Transport was not at risk from exposure.'

'Exposure to having signed a contract with the son of a known Russian gangster.'

'Yes, but for your protection and the protection of your

legitimate business transactions. You have skills to negotiate with overseas customers that your father lacks.'

'What happens when father is told who you really are - or represent? There is a proposition, which I'm happy with, that can get around this. For you it can be the same.'

'And what's that?'

'We marry Anton. This would bring confidence to the arrangement between your father and also, Izabella for that matter. It's suggested, rather than more serious vows –that they're basic like - "friends forever," in the registry office marriage.

'I've news for you Izabella plans to return to Vladivostok.' Carin's suggestion had not really resonated.

'Marry?' You would be happy to be married to the son of a gangster?'

'Happy, because I care for you Anton. I love you.' She hoped that there were no hidden microphones. Veronica nor Mike would want to hear those words.

'I have a confession to make, Carin.'

'What's that? You're not married, are you?'

'No, nothing like that. It's just that you remember I called out Petra?'

'Do I? do I? Do I remember? It's not something a woman is likely to forget. Well, what about Petra?'

'That was it Carin. I'd got the hots for you. You were in my dream. It was you I dreamt about. Then when I realized I was acting out the dream I decided to call out Petra's name. It would have looked bad. You do realize. You weren't wanting sex or anything.'

'But, I would if we married Anton. That's it. They want it to be a marriage of convenience. To secure a place to spy on your father.'

'Not me?'

'You as well, yes.'

'Come here.' Carin got out of the chair. Anton's good arm reached out and encircled her waist.

'Can I take that as a yes, then?' asked Carin.

'Can you wait a little while longer? Anton let go to assist in levering himself out of his chair. This time when his arm went around Carin, he drew her close. There were two short kisses then a more dedicated one. Carin, breathless withdrew long enough to say.'

'That is a yes, then?'

'Yes, but I'll want more than – "friends forever," in the wedding vows.'

'Me too,' replied Carin.

It was marvellous. Carin felt like shouting out "marvellous." Veronica would be "off her back," when she texted the word "yes," as directed. She'd wait a bit. Make out that an agreement had been drawn up. Separate beds, plus a bedroom exclusively hers. A laundry woman. No, that sounded like Wind in the Willows. Very old fashioned. No, there would need to be a housekeeper, who was hands on with regard to all things domestic. Washing, ironing, bathroom and toilet cleaning. Although she would cook for Anton. Certainly, be by his side at social functions. An allowance on top of her work salary. She would tell Anton that after marriage, chauffeuring would need to end. No way would she stay as driver wife.

But she would stay as perhaps Personal Assistant plus. No! That didn't sound good abbreviated. Perhaps Personal Assistant extra might be better. Children were on Carin's list, but not yet! Anton, stood back and held his arm.

'Your arm. You must be careful.'

'It's alright. But the dressing needs changing.' Carin was given a packet which contained new dressings at the hospital.

'My first aid skills come into play – again,' she said. You'll need to take your coat and shirt off. I'll assist.' Carin resisted an opportunity to stroke Anton's body and chest when exposed.

It was not the first time she'd been thwarted by circumstance. A view of Anton's chest which inspired that first longing to be pinioned against it. After the new dressing was in place and whilst helping button his shirt, she said.

'You know Carol at the Trellis and Vine?'

'Yep,'

'Well there's another girl helping out.' Carin broke away from this to say,

'Izabella has a record for woman slave smuggling. Did you know that?'

'I didn't. But I'm not shocked about it either - with Izabella, this could be possible.'

'Quite. No, it's not something she'd want you or anyone to know about.

'Meaning?'

'Well the girl. That's the one at the bar we have reason to believe is a target for Izabella.'

'For slave trading?'

'Carol?'

'No, her names Vicky'

'Are you certain?'

'We are now. Well I should say that we've been informed.'

Anton betrayed no knowledge. Carin, sat back down in the chair before she continued.

'A local girl back from Uni. Izabella's a kind of intermediary, who gets paid for setting up the kidnap. Payments to an account in her name have been traced.

'Will the fact that the payment can be traced be sufficient for the authorities to take her in?'

'Not necessarily. You understand Anton that it might not be in the interests of the state to actually, prosecute Izabella. As we understand it, they just want this young woman protected. Saved from being taken out of the country to apparently the Middle East.'

'That's good of them. Surely she should be given police protection.'

'If only, it was that simple. No, there has been so much disruption in the country over the EU. To leave or not to leave, that the government have given instructions to keep this kidnapping attempt under wraps. The last thing they want is for the public to be aware that British women are being taken for sex slaves.

'So, it's alright for eastern European women to be traded across the world?'

'I didn't say that, but the last thing they want, that's government, is for it to get into the national or any news report for that matter. Here or across the world. It would be dynamite. We have an international team of hackers shutting down sites that might be high risk.

'You mean Izabella will likely be paid and nothing more will happen.'

'That's how I understand it.'

'Are you really sure you do want to marry into this family Carin?'

'Don't you want to marry me Anton?'

'Of course, I do.' Anton tried to get up, but Carin could see that the way he grabbed hold of his injured arm that he was in pain. She stood up and held his good hand.

'That's alright then,' and knelt forward to kiss hiss cheek, before she said,

'Anton, I have serious concerns about the immediate safety of this girl Vicky.'

'Can we have lunch together here?'

'In this bedroom?'

'You can get George to agree to that better than I can.'

'I'll phone reception.

'And you'll understand shortly why I need to leave to go and look after this young woman.'

174

# Chapter 33

# Danny Helps Out

It wasn't until Carin was back in the Range Rover that Carin contacted Veronica.

'I'll need uniform back up.'

'Whatever's decided, you must remain apart from any confrontation, you understand Carin. Don't get overly involved. You're working on a hunch more than anything. You could arrive at this post office and the Chinese Motor Homers could be quietly drinking tea. The girl out riding the horse as she regularly does and then what?'

'I still think they should be under closer surveillance than just having a tracker device fitted. It's Friday and even if they leave on their own, they need monitoring.'

'Why do you think that a tracker was fitted? And here's some more up to date info – they have diplomatic immunity. They can, in due course, enter the embassy and – just disappear. And anyway, what do you intend to do when you get there? At this Post Office in this rural backwater?'

'To get peace of mine. Not least because it does now seem likely that they shot Anton.

'Right, have you anything else to report?'

'Yes.' There was a slight pause.

'Was that a "Yes," as in? ---'

'It was.'

'That's such wonderful news.'

'And where is he now?'

'Resting at the Pub.'

'Go to the post office and check the situation out. You can then return to be with your future husband. Look, with this tracking device on the Motor Home. We can get the traffic police to stop the vehicle on some pretext. We'll let Royal Mail know that you're visiting. You can show that issued inspector of police identity warrant. Well done Carin. I'll want to be at that registry office.'

Carin, started up the Range Rover and set the postcode of the sub post office into the sat nav, which followed country lanes to reach West Frampton post office. A traffic police car was parked several hundred yards away from the post office door. There was no obvious connection.

Carin, checked lipstick in the driver's mirror and whispered 'Thanks Veronica."

She was parked in the road which led down to the back field and acknowledged the patrol car's presence with a discrete hand raise. On the hill top the lower field became visible together with stables and concrete area. There was no Motor Home. A bell rang overhead when she opened the post office door. On the right were racks of cards together with spinners and various items displayed. A range of sweet packets and everyday items. Envelopes, wrapping paper, labels, pads and pens came into view as she approached the counter.

'Good afternoon can I be of assistance?' Annette popped up from behind the counter with a mail wallet in her hands.

'I'm expecting the postman, any minute.'

'Inspector Carin Hanson. I believe you're also, expecting me.'

'Yes, I guessed that was who you were.' An identity warrant, held open at the counter window, was briefly inspected. Although assigned to security services Carin needed, at times, a public identity and was given a rank that would get immediate respect and response.

'The motor home has left?'

'Oh, has it. I've been busy. So polite. I wish all motor home visitors were like those two. No trouble. Chinese, but their

English was perfect.' She said. The bell clanged again by the door. Danny, in open shirt, shorts and phone entered.

'I'm not quite ready, yet, Danny.' Carin, realized that he must be the Danny talked about in the Trellis and Vine. Carin made sure by speaking his name.

'Do you know Vicky at Linton Farm, Danny?'

'Yes, the farm is on my round. She's here now - isn't she Annette? He stopped to look at a card on a spinner.

'She'll be out on Cleopatra by now,' said Annette.

'Are you sure?' Carin needed to know.

'No, but Vicky doesn't waste any time. She'll be cantering through the fields and then back through the bridle path.' Carin wanted more assurance.

'I'd like to have your assistance Danny.' Carin produced her identity card.

'Right. I'll see whether I can help. What's it you want to know?

'At the moment, Danny I'd like to know whether Cleopatra is in her stable.'

'No problem, be back shortly, Annette. I'll shoot down in the van and have a look.'

'That'll be a start,' Carin said more to herself than the other two. After the van started. Carin said,

'I might need Danny.'

'How's that. He's a job of work to do?'

'Ongoing investigations. I can't say.'

'Such excitement for these parts. A police investigation.' Annette, sat at the counter and filled in paperwork. It was quiet inside, save for a determined clunk of the second hand from the large wall clock.

'You don't ride yourself?' Asked Carin.

'I did, but I've so much going on. Horses need exercise and Vicky comes across three times a week.

Tuesday, Wednesday and Friday. Up until this week I'd

hoped to sell Cleopatra, but it fell through. Danny was lined up to drive the lorry to the freighters, with Vicky. I'm not sure he knows its cancelled.'

'Where was the horse going to.'

'Middle East, but there was delay with vaccinations, documents etc and the buyer withdrew.'

The postal van returned and Danny entered.

'Horse's still in the stable. No sign of Vicky. What does that mean?'

'Look Danny I might want you to help me further. I'll be back.' Carin stepped outside on to the pavement and closed the door to the post office and phoned for assistance.

'Veronica? – Mike.'

'Mike, there's a situation come up with the Chinese and that Motor Home. A pause.

'You know about this?

'You do. They've left and I'm concerned that they've taken the young woman. She should be out exercising the horse and it's still stabled.'

'Yes. She was on that list site for persons wanted for slave purchase. Listings have been taken down, I know, but we need to check out the Motor Home. Preferably before it gets anywhere near Bristol airport.' Another pause.

'You'll stop it and let me know - Okay, great.' Carin stepped back inside and heard Danny say,

'Carol told me. I wanted to talk to Vicky about it. And now she's not here.' They were discussing the sale cancellation.

'Danny, we're concerned for Vicky.'

'Bet your life I'm as well.'

'I've back up down the road. We believe she might have been kidnapped.' Carin turned to Annette. 'You definitely saw Vicky when she arrived?'

'Of course, She called in for the key to the stables. She was happy. Happy that the sale had fallen through and that she could carry on riding Cleopatra. This sounds ridiculous.'

'Miss Hastings I can assure that it's not!'

'Danny can you lock your van up and leave the keys here. To stop any questions, I want you- Annette to phone the postal depot and say that Danny's got trouble with his van.'

'I can do that, but the post won't go anywhere?'

'I've no worries on that score.' Said Danny. It's Vicky's safety that matters now.

'This is very irregular.'

'I won't argue with that Annette, but this young woman's safety could depend on it. The Motor Home has a tracker and instructions have been given for it to be stopped. If possible before it gets on to the Motorway.'

'Wait here,' she said to Danny. A signal for the patrol car to draw closer was made from the hill top. A bearded police constable looked out from the open window.

'What's up Marm?'

'I want you to access this number.' She held up her phone with the lit number for operations regarding the tracking of the Motor Home. "This number." There's a vehicle track in place. Stay online. They'll give details when they've caught it. I'll be in the post office. Let me know, will you?'

'Can we know more? His companion, a young police constable sat in the passenger seat asked and looked across expectantly.

'No. Not until you can tell me that the vehicle is found and stopped. Got that.'

'Yes Marm.' Carin returned to the post office.

'They can't send anyone out for an hour,' said Annette. 'That's my dispatch delayed.' Danny was unworried by this.

'Who would want to Kidnap Vicky?' I mean how can they do this?'

'With great difficulty is our intention,' said Carin. Although, she realized that Vicky could easily be on the missing persons list, if the Motor Home got to the airport before extra security was in place there. A private jet would quickly whisk her out of the country, with suitable documentation in place. Annette might have failed with the provision of papers for Cleopatra, but the trader or traders would ensure that they had the right papers for an attractive woman that they'd bought.

Shortly afterwards there was a tap on the post office door. The bearded police officer pushed the door half open.

'That Motor Home's been caught Marm. We've got the location.'

'Okay, I'll have that from you. We'll follow there, but independently.'

'I've written it down for you.' He walked further in and handed Carin a card.

'Thanks. When you're there say that I've Danny with me to act as identification. I don't want to be visible. Danny, you can bring Vicky over to my car, okay.'

'I don't really understand what's going on, but I'll come with you, certainly if Vicky's in any danger

It was while they were following the police car that Carin explained about the Motor Home.

'The two Chinese are not just tourists. I can't tell you more about it Danny, but we're concerned that they're the kidnappers.'

'Why. I mean why has Vicky been kidnapped?'

'I'll try to explain, as best I can. Apparently, a certain Middle eastern prince became infatuated with Vicky when at uni. We don't know details. Vicky might not even have known about him. Recently we obtained information about the possible kidnap. Again, I'm unable to say more about where this information came from. We now believe Vicky has been taken hostage in the Motor Home.' A message came through from the lead police vehicle.'

'Marm, we've stopped near to the Motor Home. They've made a routine inspection of the outside of the vehicle. How are they to proceed?'

'Are you still in your vehicle.'

'Yes Marm.'

'Stay there, for now. Have they entered the cabin space?'

'No. They've only spoken with the driver?'

'Peaceable entry without recourse to armed response is first approach.'

'Emphasis that this normal procedure'

'Yes Marm. Sergeant Tranchard's Motorway Traffic's by the door.'

'Marm,' a deeper voiced response came through.

'Sergeant I'd like you to ask for entry to the cabin space.'

'Should be able to manage that, Marm. Now we've support. The Chinese guy claims to have diplomatic immunity.'

'On the basis of good diplomatic relations request entry

then. Carin spotted the Motor Home at this point in a layby.

'Armed response is to remain in vehicle for now. Keep online. I'm drawing in behind. Civilian Range Rover, dark blue Reg TR19 MVT.'

'Got you, Marm,' came back the reply from the response vehicle. The Range Rover was stopped thirty feet behind the armed response with no apparent connection, but in view of the blue and white motor Home.

'Proceed Sergeant. The two of you first to go in.'

'Will do.'

'This is where you come in Danny. You've heard what's proposed. We don't expect resistance.'

'Vicky's inside that Motor Home?'

'Pretty certain, yes. I would like you to be there when she emerges.'

'On my own?'

'No. Response will be with you.' Carin returned to call response.

'Sergeant,'

Yes, Marm, still here.'

'Good.'

'I've Danny with me. A friend of the young woman, Vicky Ledley. Once Sergeant Tranchard gains entry I want you to take Danny over to make identification and hopefully reassure this young woman. We'll take her with us.'

'And the owner occupants of said Motor Home. Placed under arrest, Marm?'

'That's tricky.'

'In what way?'

'If what they say is true and have diplomatic immunity then they're likely to be known about at the Chinese embassy. We need to tread carefully. I'll send Danny over to fetch the young woman.'

'Yes Marm, right you are.'

'You're okay about this Danny

'Yep, of course.' Danny went to open the passenger door.

'Hold on.' A few minutes passed and then the traffic constable stepped out followed by Vicky, and a slim, indignant looking Chinese woman in jeans and blazer. The driver of the response vehicle opened his door.

'Go now Danny.' Danny went across and joined the officer. Vicky with a relieved look on her face stood next to Sergeant Trenchard. On spotting Danny, she called out.

'What are you doing here? I don't understand what's going on.' Vicky pointed to the Chinese woman, now stood next to her companion.

'She, they, took me away in this. It was to test the engine, she said, then we'd return to the post office, but we didn't.' There followed a heated conversation with the two Chinese. The woman appeared to berate her driver companion.

'Are you alright, though Miss?'

'Yes. I've not been physically attacked, if that's what you mean.'

'We're over there Vicky. I'm with a police inspector. Danny pointed to where Carin was parked.

'She's driven me from the post office.'

'Are you're alright to go with this gentleman now. It's right what he's told you. He's with a female police inspector. you're okay to go with?'

'Danny, yes. I'd like to go back to Cleopatra.'

'Cleopatra?'

'Cleopatra's the horse I was about to exercise, before I stepped into this.' Vicky pointed to the open door of the Motor Home.

'Right Miss, as you say. we'll be seeing to these two from now on. Vicky looked more perplexed than scared as they walked to where Carin was parked. When they drew near Carin lowered the window, smiled,

'Would you like to sit next to me Vicky.'

'Where are we?' She asked.

'Not that far from the post office.'

'Oh, I've sort of lost any idea of time.' When she closed the car door, she collapsed sobbing into her arms.

'It's alright, you're safe now.' Carin, stroked her hair.

'That woman showed me pictures of a palace and was saying how would I like to live there Then the police siren sounded and she started to put the photos away. She told be to stay quiet. She'd said that they would return to the stable after the engine was tested. But they weren't going to do that, were they?' Danny now sat behind was surprised when Carin said.

'They perhaps might have been about to return.' Danny caught Carin's strict look. Carin considered that the true nature of this incident best withheld from Vicky, at this point. She opened the glove box. Vicky grabbed some tissues and pulled the sun visor down.

'And why, I mean how's Danny with you.'

'We were worried about you Vicky,' said Danny.

'Cleo was there in the stable, and there was no sign of you.'

'But how did you know I was in the Motor Home?'

'I can't go into details Vicky, but we were already tracking this vehicle, for security reasons. Again, Carin turned to Danny. This time she placed a finger to her lips, whilst Vicky was inspecting what remained of her make up

'Would you like to be taken back to Linton Farm?'

'What about Cleopatra. I haven't taken her out?' she paused in dabbing her face.

'Right, we'll return to West Frampton Post Office, then.'

'But what about me?' Asked Danny. 'How am I to get back to civilization?'

I left the key to my van. They've likely taken it back to the main office.' This brought a smile from Vicky.

'I wouldn't call Brodham civilization any more than West Frampton, Danny. I'll take you back into town. I've got father's pick up.' Vicky was now more relaxed. Carin decided not to talk further about the Motor Home incident. By way of distraction she said,

'I understand Cleopatra's to stay at Miss Hasting's stables. I expect you're pleased about that...?

# Chapter 35

# Report Back to Base

Carin stopped in a layby on her way back to the Trellis and Vine. She caught, from the post office window, sight of Danny, who helped Vicky into Cleopatra's saddle. It was a good move to take Danny with her. She considered this whilst on the phoned to Mike from the Range Rover. Mike's first words were.

'That girl's been·taken back, and now we've to explain to uniform branch that we're not taking action.'

'Not taking action?' replied Carin.

'These two are not really tourists, Carin and the government is in the midst of securing a contract with a major Chinese company. There's no way, that they'll want a run in with the Chinese Embassy. But don't worry yourself about that.' Carin resented the patronizing tone of her boss, but knew that overseas political consideration could inform on whether legal action would be taken against certain foreign nationals, in the interest of international diplomacy. Not information available for the public domain, though. Her thoughts, now and even in the midst of the Motor Home chase, were about Anton, she guiltily admitted.

'We'll be in touch. Oh, and Veronica tells me that you're about to secure marriage with Anton Carter.'

'Secure? Not sure that's the right word.

'It'll need to be a registrar office marriage, you realize. We can provide necessary evidence for a separation and divorce, in due course.'

'Thanks for that reassurance, Mike - appreciate.

It was still light when Carin returned through the door of

the Trellis and Vine. Anton was approaching the bar, with his arm sling removed when she walked in. She'd not messaged.

'The first words to Anton from George were.'

'I hope the Polo injury is not too severe.'

'Carin was able to update the situation for Anton by saying,

'One of my new responsibilities looking after a wounded polo player.'

'Anton quick to realize the story told to George,' join in with

'Yes, but it's not that serious. Hope to be back in the saddle on my next visit, George.'

'Glad to, hear that Mr Carter. May I ask are you with us tonight for an evening meal?' Anton, looked across to Carin, who was swiping her smart phone, to appear that she was making a check on engagements.

'We really need to start out soon. There's an engagement tomorrow, Saturday.'

'Not aware of this,' Anton's raised eyebrows momentarily betrayed disbelief, before he replied to George,

'But I'm sure Carin, has everything in order. We've time for a drink?'

'Just, said Carin. Make mine a lemon and lime, though.' Whilst George was preparing a gin and tonic for Anton Carin said,

'It's still light. Let's go outside. Whilst George's back was turned, she moved closer and whispered before she kissed him – 'I've so missed you Anton.

George insisted in bringing the drinks out on a tray. They'd decided to sit at a table for two beneath a scatter of very old vine branches, that made it appear like a tree hut when viewed from the bar area.

'The girls safe, you'll be pleased to know. The plan was to smuggle her away in a Motor Home. Two Chinese with diplomatic immunity.'

'In your uniformed branches custody now then?'

'Not exactly. It's not likely to lead to prosecution. Traffic stopped the vehicle shortly after they drove away with Vicky inside to view the room space of their Motor Home. Vicky, then told that they were testing the engine, before they finally left.They should've been stopped at customs.'

'No, it's complicated, Anton. Main priority was that she was safe. But how's your arm?'

'It throbs with pain all the time.' He made to wince when he spoke. But pain killers numb it a bit. No, it's not that bad.

'I feel bad about leaving you.'

'Good,' he said. 'I wouldn't have it otherwise.' His hand from the good arm reached across, and Carin reached out to take hold of it and cupped it between both hands.

'And Miss Carin Hanson, shortly to be Mrs Carter what is this appointment I have tomorrow?'

'I've arranged to visit father.'

'Ah, there's a thing. Does he know?'

'Sort of, I think he could. He brought me after mother died.

'And what do you mean by that exactly, Miss Hanson?'

'When he knew that you'd lent me the use of a Range Rover he said – "No man lends his car to just any woman." I remember him smiling quietly to himself afterwards, but thought nothing of it.

'You're not just any woman.'

'I might have been. Just one woman in a stream of Personal Assistants.'

'You never were and certainly aren't now.'

'Here's to my appointment with Jerry. We have met. At Henry's farewell party he came with Simon - Simon! How's he going to take this?'

'He's not in my life now Anton. He kind of hasn't really been there for some-time. You're not worried about Simon?'

'Only if you are Carin,'

'Well I'm not. Hey look she pointed up at the crescent moon. 'It's tilted on its back. That means we can relax, as well.'

'You're not superstitious are you Carin?'

'I believe phases of the moon can affect us. It certainly can affect a woman's cycle and that's not forgetting the rise and fall of tides.'

'So, I've an appointment with your father, tomorrow. He knows about it?'

'Not completely. But it concerns you and me.' Anton finally arrives at the reason.

'Of course. Now you've frightened me. He could say no. He might not want his beautiful daughter marrying into a family like mine.

# The end

# Also by Sam Grant

Please check out these other publications by Sam Grant, author of River Escape:

*Atlantic Hijack* (978-1-78222-291-0). Apprentice engineer Mike Peters is finding his feet amongst a cast of nautical characters as the Albany Princess voyages to Montevideo. But the ship's personnel are not all that they make themselves out to be, as revealed during a rapidly unravelling hijack in the South Atlantic.

*Dancing on the Beach* (978-1-78222-431-0). A romantic thriller. Achieved a most popular read category on promotekdbook.com in 2016.

*Poems with themed notes* (978-1-78222-464-8). An anthology of forty poems .

*Galactic Mission*, 2017 (978-1-78222-512-6). A science fiction novel. Listed, with pre-views on Amazon.

*River Escape* (978-1-78222-574-4) is the sequel to *Atlantic Hijack*. An individual novel, which continues to follow the sea career of Mike Peters.

url: amazon.com/author/grantsam

Available from all good booksellers - if not in stock, please order using the ISBN.

Request from the author:

If you enjoy reading *Persuasion's Price*, please post a short review on your bookseller's web page where you purchased the book.

Lightning Source UK Ltd.
Milton Keynes UK
UKHW020303130919
349657UK00009B/457/P

9 781782 226871